www.gideon-burrows.com

The Spiral

To Nikki McCarthy

Published by Gideon Burrows t/a ngo.media,
75 Gurney Road, Stratford, E15 1SL

ALSO BY GIDEON BURROWS

Fiction

Portico: The Social Media Thriller

The Illustrator's Daughter

The Spiral

Future Shop

Locked In

Ninja of Light: Hako Ninja 1 (as G D Burrows)

Ninja of Steel: Hako Ninja 2 (as G D Burrows)

Non-fiction

Your Life In The Metaverse

Metaverse 101

Glioblastoma: A guide for patients and loved ones

Living Low Grade: A patient guide

This Book Won't Cure Your Cancer

Men Can Do It: Why Men Don't Do Childcare

Chilli Britain: A Hot and Fruity Adventure

Martin & Me

THE SPIRAL

GIDEON BURROWS

1

Reggie Ross hit the woman. He killed her.

Strictly speaking Reggie Ross didn't hit her. Strictly speaking he didn't kill the woman.

But for the rest of his life, Reggie Ross would always have to say to himself: I hit and killed that woman. He'd have to take it to his own deathbed.

Thirty years driving trains and Reggie Ross had never had a 'one under'. Then, in his last week on the job before retirement, his very last week for God's sake, he got one. His leaving drinks were already organised at The Barrowboy & Banker at London Bridge. Then today, this morning, he'd hit and killed a woman.

A one under.

Something every train driver knows they'll get at least once in their career. Often more. A jumper. A suicide. A faller. Someone pushed. *A one under*.

It took about five seconds for Reggie Ross to find out if the pretty girl standing too close to the other end of the platform at St Paul's was to be his first and only one under.

It was five seconds, but it seemed to stretch for five hours.

Reggie had only done one switch of the Central Line so far that day. It was an early start. His first train, 5.00 a.m. from Hainault via Bank to Ealing. His first journey went without a problem, not even an unexpected stop light. But on his second loop. Well, that was different.

When you're a Tube driver, most of what you see is the dark rails swinging around corners, ever trying to converge in the distance. But they never quite make it. Those haunting lines and the blip-blip-blip of white lights that pass. They can send a driver into a kind of trance.

Sometimes, Reggie couldn't tell whether he was awake or asleep. It was a welcome feeling of distance from the world, but the darkness could also give you a chill. After three decades driving London Underground trains, Reggie still secretly welcomed the reassurance of the circle of brightness ahead as a station hurtled towards him.

Then he'd gently come out of his trance, let his right hand roll forwards against the pressure of the driving handle and ease off the gas. He'd let out a comfortable sigh as the carriages rolled neatly into the station. He always prided himself on stopping in the correct place without a touch on the emergency brake.

Reggie reckoned he'd spent about a quarter of his life under the surface. Only miners beat that.

His dad had been a railway driver too, but above the surface. He'd worked the West Coast Mainline after the war. There were materials - coal, steel, bricks - to be carried from the Black Country to London to help with rebuilding the capital.

Good steady work for his dad, and that was back in the days when there were jobs for life. Reggie had been lucky.

His dad's connections in the Union had helped him get a job on the Underground and once he was behind the dead-man's handle, it was hard for any government, or New Labour consortium of quasi-government companies, to prise him out again.

Now Reggie was nearing 60, no one would dare even try. What with age discrimination and RMT Union threats of strikes if anyone even so much as threatened new pension arrangements or to privatise the lines again.

For Reggie it was a simple life. And good money. He'd never really had any official training: it seemed back then they just put you into the driver's carriage, pointed towards the tunnel and sent you on your way.

More recently, of course, he had to attend brand awareness days, training on customer relations, courses on health and safety for drivers. They were only slightly more work than driving a Tube train, and most often seemed to be presented by those who looked like they'd arrived in taxis and never used the Tube in their life. At least Reggie got paid for the training, and who knows: health and safety training could do no harm.

There were presentations about communication with fellow Underground staff. About spotting anything dangerous, like a platform that was too raucous (a football match has just finished); or too crowded (radio up to surface level to close some inward ticket barriers, slow up entries). And classes on spotting something unusual. These days that meant terrorism. A discarded package. Someone who looked out of place. Didn't seem to belong.

See It. Say It. Sorted.

The girl attracted Reggie's attention because, at this time in the morning, a single young woman waiting for a Tube train *was* unusual. Particularly at St Paul's. At this time, it was mostly only big men in paint-smudged overalls and grubby reinforced boots who would get on, and then only at the far-out stations. They'd be on their way to or from one of the next skyscrapers they were throwing up between the last ones they'd worked on in the city. Builders and labourers got *off* the train at St Paul's at this time. People rarely boarded in the financial district this early *at all*. And definitely not a young woman.

Alone.

The girl wasn't dressed for 6.15 a.m. She wore an orange skirt hitched above the knees, a light blue jacket - was it denim? - buttoned up to the neck. Her hair seemed limp, but not untidy. A little makeup, but smudged. Had she been out all night, and on her way home?

Possibly. But that only happened on a Saturday and Sunday morning. All-nighters coming home from clubbing in central London. But they usually came home in groups of three or four. And anyway, this wasn't central London.

There were no nightclubs in the financial district. On the weekend most of the pubs weren't open during the day, let alone at night.

But there was something else. Something about how the girl was dressed. Something Reggie couldn't put his finger on. Her head dipped. From the side Reggie could see a blank distant look on her face. She wasn't reading one of those posters that curved up the inside of station tunnels. She was looking down onto the rails. Reggie looked to the area where her eyes led, then back to the platform where she was standing.

That was it. The something else. He could just make out the low pink glow of her grubby toenails underneath the Tube station lights. A few inches from the edge of the train platform, the wrong side of the yellow line.

A pretty girl at the wrong time, in the wrong place. Standing on the bumpy lines cut into the concrete platform edge. Not belonging.

And she wasn't wearing shoes.

Something was definitely wrong with this picture. And when something doesn't look right there's only one thing Reggie's driver training had taught him he should do.

He hit the brake.

2

C harles was only 30 or so steps down when he had to take his first rest. No more than a few seconds, but at least he'd got down more steps than yesterday before having to stop. He clung onto the metal bannister and took a moment to collect himself. To take a breath or two.

He waited for the twinge in his chest to calm. Charles took a hankie from his blazer pocket, removed his glasses, and wiped his brow. He stuffed the hankie back into the pocket and then felt in the blazer on the other side for a little cylinder of pills. There they were, under his leather notebook.

Charles didn't *want* to take the staircase down to the Northern Line that day. But it was doctor's orders.

They'd always been walkers, he and Felicity. But these days, he wasn't doing the exercise he needed to stay on top of a slowly ageing heart.

"You're just starting to creak up a bit, Mr Lawrence," the doctor told him. "Do some gardening, get off the bus a little earlier, a little vacuuming. Anything to keep the joints oiled."

He'd sent him away with a prescription.

Gardening. That's what the headteacher had recommended too. Charles would be due for retirement in a couple of years. He should take some gardening leave. Take it easy until his pension kicks in. Let things die down a bit.

Charles hated gardening. All that scraping of weeds from between patio slabs, clipping a few centimetres off the side of hedges, scratching grass to get rid of the moss.

There was a proper old woman next door who'd appear every time the sun shone. She had white hair, a green puffer jacket, pink bobbled gloves and knee pads. A Gardener's World cliché. She was always out there with her secateurs or a trowel. She'd put sheets down to collect the weeds so she didn't damage her perfect lawn when tending to the flower beds. She'd use a dustpan and brush to gather up the leaves from the shrubs, the driveway, from the grass for God's sake. She'd brush the pavement outside her house, creating a little line of dust exactly where her property stopped and his began.

Charles' garden was a rough patch of grass in front of a tiny bungalow. He liked it that way. Now it was all grown over with weeds and waist height saplings from surrounding trees. He hadn't touched it for two years. Didn't intend to either. Let his uppity neighbour grumble, with her too perfect patch.

Gardening. Gardening is what old people do. People with empty lives. Old bastards who are going senile. Charles smiled, patted the notebook in his blazer, and continued downwards. Felicity had been the gardener.

He'd been going this way down since the doctor's appointment and was sure it would do him some good in the long term. He liked this staircase, even though the steps were narrow and the going was slow. There was a solid bannister to hold on to, and only a few people came this way. Most passengers didn't even know about it.

He could get the exercise he was supposed to, but take little breathers now and then without getting in the way. At the other end, the easy way down with the escalators, he had always been pushed and jostled. People would tut at him if he had to stop, even for a second.

He'd had enough of the tutting and pushing.

At the bottom of the stairs, he would board the Northern Line and go up to Euston. From there, he'd walk for ten minutes to the British Library, take tea in the café. Then he'd continue his research in the history department, making detailed notes in his little notebook.

Kings Cross Station was slightly nearer to the library, but the doctor had said every tiny snippet of extra exercise would do an extra bit of good. For his heart. For his mental health.

That was the talk these days. Mental Health. Like it wasn't okay to feel lonely. Or think back to the old days, about his friends on the submarines, with fond sadness. Can't possibly be miserable. Pull your socks up.

Everyone had to be *happy*. Everyone had to be *sociable*. Everyone had to be *friendly*.

He'd tried that. Now he was on gardening leave.

———

The Tube train halted so abruptly outside Bank Station that Giles' head bounced off the glass. He was already pressed in by some huge tourist with a guidebook and a stupid cap. His massive suitcase was squashing Giles to the side.

Why did they need so much stuff, anyway? Tourists should be banned from the Tube, during the morning commute at least. Most of them could walk between Tube stations anyway, if they could be bothered to look at Google maps.

The stuffy train carriage was full of school kids, of course. The girls mocked each other, shouting across the gangway in whiny voices. The boys were talking tough, especially when the girls were watching. They gathered in a clump, bumping into Giles even though there were sprinkles of empty seats they should shift to. White kids talking Black. Calling each other *bro*, waving their hands like rappers. Stupid oversized bright white trainers. So white they hurt Giles' eyes. The kids' voices wheedled their way into his head, ramping his headache up a few more notches.

Giles took another swig of Lucozade and swallowed past the dryness in his throat. So much for a hangover cure. The sickly fizz, with the background taste of TCP, was supposed to knock out the fug. But this hangover was the real deal.

Tequila, wasn't it? Gin and tonics? Definitely cocktails, and of course a line or two. Champagne later in the casino. That's on top of the four pints of European lager straight after work.

A voice came over the tannoy, all chummy cockney accent, *we're in this together.*

"Sorry folks. As per previous, we had an incident on the line earlier this morning. We're all backed up. I'll get you all into Bank Station just as soon as I can. Shouldn't be any more than a few minutes."

"Shit," said Giles. A school teacher looked across at him, but Giles stared him down. Every couple of months some selfish idiot would throw themselves onto the line.

Another three minutes. The train had been stop-start all along the Central Line since he'd got on at Snaresbrook, where he shared digs with some friends from his Cambridge college.

The train lurched forward, then stopped, then lurched forward again. Bile rose from Giles' stomach with the sway, but he kept the Lucozade down and belched behind his hand.

The doors finally slid open and Giles kicked past the tourist's suitcase and stepped onto the platform. Without taking a break, he turned left, heading against the crowd towards the staircase down to the Northern Line.

It was his usual route to Bank, then one stop under the river to his office in The Shard at London Bridge. Most of the others went the long way via the escalators at the other end of the platform. As if a few steps were more than they could handle.

Benny fell back gratefully, allowed his whole body to go limp and be enveloped by the seat. He leant his head right back and rested it against the window behind. The stretch in his neck felt good. He closed his eyes and enjoyed first the low vibrations as the Tube doors closed, then the deeper rocking as the carriage got underway. This is how they rock babies to sleep.

He opened his eyes, lifted his head and glanced up at the long red Tube line outlined on the ceiling ahead of him. He counted across. This was Stratford, so it would go Mile End, Bethnal Green, Liverpool Street... he stopped naming the stations after Bank and just counted the little red squares sitting on the line. Eighteen stops until East Acton. Forty five minutes at least, maybe an hour. Not long enough to sleep, but unbearably long to keep awake. He closed his eyes again, put his head back, and tried to get comfortable. Only the sound of some school kids at the other end of the carriage might disturb him, but he was too tired to be bothered. The train slowed as it pulled into Mile End, the doors opened, the doors shut, the train speeded up again.

Seventeen more.

It had been the usual story last night. Benny had climbed out of bed in the tiny room in a flat he shared with others he'd been put together with on the Programme. He didn't really *know* them. Didn't really want to. He slept through the day, then worked at night. They, the other way around.

He opened his bedroom door quietly and entered the bathroom. He brushed his teeth and splashed his face, staring down into a filthy limescale-caked plug hole. He looked into the mirror at eyes that veined with thin red threads of tiredness. He ran the back of his hand against the rough stubble on his cheek. He really ought to have taken a shower and a shave to wake up a bit, but he didn't have any of those crappy plastic shaving blades left. It was a long time since he'd had the money for decent blades.

Back in his room, Benny had pulled on jeans heavy with paint and oil. He picked up and sniffed the t-shirt that had been lying on the floor, then squeezed himself into it and buttoned up a lumberjack shirt over the top. He chose some new socks from the pile because once his feet sweated in those heavy work boots, his blisters would get worse and he'd end up limping around the site.

Benny had taken the last Tube out of East Acton and sat eating a dry bread roll and sipping from a bottle of water he'd filled up from the tap in the bathroom. All the building was taking place in the East End now. Guys like Benny had to follow the work, even if it was the other side of London. He hated going back east.

The Programme had hooked him up with the agency. The agency had hooked him up with some site safety training. Now he had to go where they told him.

Mixing sand and concrete all night at a waste ground, turning it into a car park near Leyton. Hauling bricks up and down scaffolds at Bethnal Green. For the last two weeks, he'd been ripping up broken paving stones and cracked concrete, wheelbarrowing the hardcore to skips at a newbuild close to the Olympic Park.

The doors opened. Liverpool Street. The doors closed.

Bernard Harris. Benny. The limp guy at the Programme had called him Benny on the first day when he'd flounced into the centre with a smile on his face, swinging a clipboard. An identity card hung from a pink lanyard around his neck, the words Unite written repetitively along its length.

Benny. It was meant in a friendly way, but the tone the guy used as he went through the paperwork – *now Benny, let's see how we can really help you reach your future potential* – irritated him. *We* weren't going to help Bernard at all. And Bernard didn't have any future potential. He doubted the 22-year-old in front of him had ever smoked a spliff, let alone knew what cocaine looked like.

But after three or four brainstorming sessions – *let's just think blue skies, Benny, no rules, just imagine, blue skies* – Bernard had got to like the guy.

Call me Stevie. He liked the way Stevie would laugh at himself, be rude about the other staff at the project, and still had the innocence to think he really could help someone like Bernard.

Make that Benny. New name, new start.

The agency had been much more detached. Paperwork. Distaste. The girl assigned to him always had the attitude that she was doing Benny a huge favour. Just be grateful there are people like me around. Stevie would have *bitched* about her. A *Tart in a Tiara*, he'd have said.

"We'll only be able to give you a day's notice, a couple of days at most. But it's work. So get some tough clothes, just turn up and do what they tell you to do. You'll be able to hang on to your benefits as long as you keep showing up, so you better get used to late nights."

Benny had nodded and smiled at what he thought was her being friendly. But she'd gone back to ticking boxes on the form in front of her.

"Okay, off you go," she said. "I'll call you when something comes in."

Moorgate.

"You're Bernard Harris?" the foreman at Stratford had asked last Monday, checking his clipboard. It felt like Benny's life had been one of being passed from clipboard to clipboard in the last year. "Good. You've got your boots. You can get your helmet and gloves from that mobile over there. Tea break at 3 a.m., same unit. A bloke in the pit will give you something to do until then."

"They call me Benny," he had said.

But the foreman wasn't listening anymore. He'd already turned away. Just like the others. Keep your head down, thought Benny. Just keep your head down and carry on.

When the Tube doors opened at Bank, Megan was first out of the carriage. She'd already stood and worked her way through the rocking train as soon as it had left Liverpool Street.

She tried not to be one of those typical Londoners, always in a rush even though they weren't going anywhere special. Grunting if you forgot to stand on the right going up escalators. But these were special circumstances. The train was moving extra slow because of the incident the driver kept talking about. What would it look like at Rank and Tudor Chambers if she arrived even five minutes late for her second interview at the legal firm?

Arrive at least 10 minutes before. That was the unspoken rule. Not 20 minutes early, that showed desperation. Not five minutes early either. That was too blasé. On time or even a minute late, well you didn't really want the job, did you?

As soon as Megan shot off the train, she realised she was in the wrong place. The exit was at the opposite end of the platform and was already filling up with people waiting to get around the corner and into the escalator area. She cursed.

She'd never worked in London. Hadn't even been to the capital that much. Only shopping, really. Her dad wasn't even very keen on that. But after college she'd swung a job as a financial secretary and general dogsbody at a local solicitor's in Epping. She'd studied for three years part-time to be a legal secretary because that was where the money was. But she had had no luck at all getting an actual legal job.

Until now and this second interview. Would Dad be proud if she got it? Not likely. And now her chances of landing the job at Rank and Tudor were trickling away, stuck behind this crowd.

It would peter out, Megan knew that, but did she have time to let it?

She spied a man in the deep blue uniform of the London Underground. He'd just announced (again) that the Central Line was all backed up and was replacing the radio handset back on his belt.

"Hi, can you help me?" she said as calmly as she could. "I'm late. Is there another way to the Northern Line?"

The station announcer looked up at the crowd waiting at the end of the platform and returned to look at Megan. She had failed to ask as calmly as she'd thought. The announcer had clearly heard the desperation in her voice and offered a thin, sympathetic smile.

"If you head to the other end, you could go down the stairs," he said. "It'll probably take as long as getting past this lot though, but it's worth a try." He looked down for a moment at her flat shoes. "At least you're not in high heels."

He chuckled, though Megan didn't know why.

Megan headed back the way she had just come. Maybe it would take as long, but at least she was doing something.

I take decisions and act on them. I use my initiative, act quickly when the circumstances require it. It's really a question of getting the balance right, isn't it?

Megan walked quickly and cursed her slow start. She didn't run. Who could run in this bloody skirt? She'd bought it for the interview. In Heals it had looked good. Smart and businesslike, attractive too. But in front of the mirror after an early breakfast, she realised she'd been kidding herself. It was way too tight, a size too small, at least. It bulged in all the wrong places, particularly the *worst* place.

She'd pulled it on and off four times, trying it against her usual work skirts. But they all looked way too old, too faded for a second interview. She couldn't wear the other new skirt, the one she'd bought for the first interview. That would show sloppiness, lack of ambition. She'd learned that watching The Apprentice. The new skirt it had to be.

Her dad wanted to see her, all dressed up in a new suit, before she left. He grunted, disapproving. And now she was late. She was still touching up her makeup while she waited for the train out of Epping.

Megan saw the sign for the Northern Line and headed down the narrow corridor until she found the staircase. A pale-looking man in a smart suit was standing dead still at the top, as if considering whether to take the plunge. He looked up and smiled. Almost invited her, with a nod, to pass him. She smiled back. She took a shallow breath, nipped past him and onto the stairs.

"Thanks, just in a rush," she said as she passed, throwing back a brief glance of apology.

Giles pulled the knot of his thin tie further down his chest, looking for less stuffy air on the platform and finding only the faint taste of dirt and grime. He wore a smart business suit, patent shoes, the lot. But he would not do up his top button and pull up his tie until he'd gone past security and was right there in the lift, heading to the 13th floor of The Shard.

Asswipe would be waiting, that was guaranteed. Loitering by the front desk of Fastex Commodities like a fart. He wouldn't be tapping his foot impatiently for Giles. He would just be waiting. Just so he could look up with a raised eyebrow that said: 'Mr Laws, what time do you call this?' and then he'd make a note of it in some stupid file he'd pull out next appraisal time.

Andy Asquith. His boss. He had gone to Cambridge, just

like Giles, but had made far more of it. Just 24 years old, but lords it over everyone else on the trading floor. Some milk-round had leap-frogged him over the hard grafters working the trades like Giles, and put him in prime position.

Giles had called in sick a few too many times lately. He couldn't get away with it today, even though they'd all been out last night. Asswipe had been out with them, of course. Buying drinks as if to remind everyone how much more he was paid. That his bonus was bigger than theirs.

But he always ducked out early, never followed through. He'd get them pissed enough to want to carry on into the evening, then wag his finger at them the next morning as they straggled in.

Tuesday is the new Friday. Lately the new Friday had been Wednesday and Thursday too. Friday was always Friday. That was a given.

Giles stopped at the top of the spiral staircase down to the Northern Line and tried again to shake away the pounding in his head. Took a swig of Lucozade. One hundred and twenty-eight steps. Seemed like he'd counted them every day, Monday to Friday, since starting this shitty job. When was that? Five months ago?

Winchester College for school. Then to Trinity College, Cambridge for university. Second eight in the rowing team. Extra tuition, so he managed to scrape by with a 2:2. All paid for by his *oh so lovely* parents, living the life of million-aires in the countryside, without the trouble of, say, bringing up a kid instead of packing him off to boarding school.

And all for what? Unsociable hours of hard work and peer pressure?

It wasn't the job. It was his life. He'd been on the wrong track from the start. He could have opened a coffee shop. Or become a firefighter. Or even police. Only, that's not what guys like him did. Banker. Business strategist. Consultant.

Giles didn't even know what a consultant did.

His head swam. For a moment he thought he might faint. This hangover was a killer. Could he sit down here, just for a second?

A woman in a smart cream blouse and grey A-line skirt nipped past him with a smile. He welcomed the relief of not having to go down just now. He smiled back and stepped aside to let her through. Be my guest, you look much more keen to get on with your life.

He looked at his watch. It showed ten to nine and that he was going to be late.

What a shame.

Bank.

Benny opened his eyes again. The doors had swished open, but they hadn't closed again to complete the rhythm. The interruption had pushed him out of half-sleep. Passengers were poking their heads out of the doors. They were glancing up towards the front carriage as if they could catch the driver's attention and remind him of his job.

"Ladies and gents," a muffled voice came over the tannoy in response. "Sorry to inform that I've just been told this train is stopping here because of an earlier disruption on the line. Repeat, this train will stop here. You are advised to step onto the platform and either wait for the next train, or to continue your journey by another route. All change here."

The Tube train wasn't particularly packed. Though to Benny it felt like late at night, it was really just approaching nine in the morning. A few passengers muttered under their breath, but most just stepped from the train in familiar resignation.

Benny rose, picked up his small leather toolbag and stepped onto the platform. He used a Tube map on the wall to consider his options, struggling to share the space with an overweight man in a cap. His stomach bulged over his waistband and meaty pink arms flapped out of his short-sleeved shirt as he traced lines on the map with fat fingers.

Whichever way it went, it was going to be an extra 20 minutes, maybe even half-an-hour's travelling time, before Benny reached East Acton. Only then could he could take a shower and go to bed in a room with windows too bright for him to sleep properly.

He could try to swing round in a triangle on the Tube lines, and end up back on the Central Line at Holborn or Tottenham Court Road. But who knew where the blockage started and ended? It could be just as slow further up. He traced the black line northwards from Bank.

He could get onto the Northern Line, change at Moorgate onto the pink line - what is that, the Hammersmith and City Line? - then at least he wouldn't have to change again until it had worked its way round to Wood Lane Station. Then, if he was knackered, he could switch back on the Central Line and go one stop to East Acton. But considering the Programme accommodation was half-way between the two, he might as well get off and walk the rest. If his body had anything left by then.

Benny looked up and headed towards the sign for the Northern Line. His way was blocked on either side by the obese man with the cap, who was heading in the same direction, dragging a suitcase behind him.

The two went down a narrow corridor, offering Benny

even less space to go round, and they reached the top of a spiral staircase together.

Shit. This is the wrong way down. It would take an age, particularly if he had to follow this guy. But going back onto the platform, then up to the other end, then round the corridors to the escalators, would take just as long. And make his feet hurt just as much.

"Jeees, I dunno why you guys don't got no elevators," the guy muttered behind him, turning to looking at Benny for the first time. Benny nodded and offered an apologetic smile.

"Oh...," the guy said, and turned away from him.

It was an 'oh' that Benny was familiar with. The tourist had taken one look at Benny, the colour of his skin, his stubble, the builder's clothes and ever so slightly backed away.

The tourist tried to wedge his bag under one flabby arm, but it was too heavy. He'd have to bump it down. He grabbed for the handrail.

"You better go on, son," he said, wheezing, flicking his head toward the stairs below. "I don't move so fast on my feet."

"Thank you," said Benny, going around the tourist. "Listen, there is another way down. Where are you going to?"

He didn't reply. He looked unconvinced, glancing Benny up and down, eyeing his worn fingernails and mucky boots.

"There are escalators. At the other end of the platform. It'll help with the bag."

Still nothing.

"Okay, at least let me carry it down for you. I think this is a long one."

The man clutched the suitcase even tighter. "No, I'm fine. Just fine as I am. You just go on ahead, son."

The main waited.

Benny tried to smile at the guy. He had no choice but to push past the struggling man and leave him far behind. He worried his smile came out as fake as it really was. But he *was* trying. New name, new start.

"Okay, thanks a lot. Have a good day." Benny squeezed past the tourist and headed down and around the spiral, leaving him far behind.

3

M egan headed down the stairwell quickly, conscious that someone was following her five or six steps behind. Probably the friendly guy in the suit. The spiral staircase was just about wide enough for two people to go down together, but the concrete steps gradually thinned into a small wedge on the right by the time they joined the central column. It was dodgy to try it.

Megan tried to walk in the middle. She hated small spaces. Someone walking with her would be way too close. She needed space.

At least the staircase was well lit. Megan could see about eight steps in front of her before the last one ran around the corner and out of view.

The handrail was thick iron and protruded from the staircase wall, marking the boundary between brown tiles below it and dull grey ones above. The roof was plain concrete, sectioned by small round lights embedded into the ceiling. The entire space echoed with Megan's flat heels as they slapped on each step.

Her feet were chafing with each drop, but it couldn't be

much further. Then she'd be on the platform, onto the Northern Line and might just about make the interview with a few minutes to spare.

Ahead, Megan saw a brown blazer and the wispy thin grey hair of an older man moving much slower than she. For a moment, Megan backed up behind him. She didn't want to crowd him. Just like she didn't want to be crowded.

Instead, she followed him slow step by slow step as he gently rocked down the stairs, clinging tightly to the handrail. This was all she needed, extra minutes. Finally, she knew she had to move. She edged to the inside of the staircase, keeping a close eye on her footing as she passed.

"Sorry," she said. "Do you mind if I?"

"No, of course." The man's breath was a little laboured. "Do you know how much further it is?" he asked.

She stopped and looked back up at the old man. The younger man in the suit was now directly above them both.

"Sorry, I don't know," she replied. She noticed beads of sweat had gathered in the old man's thick white eyebrows. "It's not much further I'm sure."

The young man coughed, though he smiled again at Megan.

"Sorry, my boss is going to have me for breakfast."

Megan and the older man moved to the side to let him pass. Megan took a breath, to deal with feeling a little cramped with two other people so close.

"Are sure you're okay?" she asked the older man.

"Yes, I'm fine. Just taking it one step at a time. Doctor's orders."

Megan turned back down the stairs. Now the younger guy was in front of her and she was following him. At least he moved faster than the old man, who she could still hear shuffling behind her, wheezing with each step. Within ten more steps, he was out of range.

Out of mind.

Megan and the man in the suit didn't speak. Londoners never do. They carried on down as a pair without even acknowledging each other's presence. Soon, though, the man's pace seemed to have sped up. Perhaps three steps for every two Megan took.

It felt like she'd been going down for five minutes, and the man in front was edging out of view. Or maybe it was Megan who was slowing down. Now she too was panting and her calf muscles were aching. She felt like the walls were getting closer, and wondered about the last time she went to the gym. Dad didn't like her going to the gym. Mind you, Dad didn't want her to work in the City either.

She didn't remember her mum. Dad never spoke about her. Megan didn't realise she didn't have one until she'd started primary school. When she'd asked him - what was she, about five? - he'd just said she'd gone. Didn't love us enough to stay.

"Don't be asking again. End of subject."

Megan remembered crying all night. Then Dad coming in to tell her to stop being such a baby. The rest of the tears she saved for when he was out of the house: at the pub, or the betting shop, or *putting in a 'hard day's work on the tools'*.

Being from a single parent family wasn't unusual at her school. But at least the other kids seemed to know why.

She'd kept herself to herself. Only had a few friends, the neighbours close to them. Only the ones Dad had done some building work for.

Dad rarely took her to playdates, or to birthday parties. He said he didn't like the small talk.

They were a good pair, he said. We're okay by ourselves. We don't need anyone else.

But with Dad, it wasn't us. It was him. Him, with Megan doing whatever she was told. Any achievements she made at school, she kept to herself. Any choices she made about school clubs, or subjects or projects, were hers alone. Dad just wasn't interested.

He provided food, didn't he? A roof over her head? Her school uniform? He let her play on the street with the neighbours' kids. The TV licence cost a fortune too. What else did she want?

When Megan had her first period, it was the school nurse who explained. She'd kept the sanitary towels she used at home hidden, wrapped them in toilet paper, then dumped them in public bins on the way to school.

Megan looked at her watch. There was no way she was going to make her appointment now. Even at the bottom of the stairs, she'd have to find the correct platform and wait for the next Northern Line train. Perhaps if she went back up again, she could go the way the other passengers were headed. In fact, she could go right to surface level and call the Chambers' reception and apologise for being late. Ask them to keep her interview slot open. She stopped and checked her phone.

No reception.

"Excuse me," she called to the young man in front of her. She could now only see his shoulders and the top of his head as he continued beneath her. "Excuse me," she said again.

The man turned, a look of slight impatience.

"Sorry, but have you any idea how long the staircase goes on for. It feels like we've been going down forever."

"It's exactly one hundred and twenty-eight steps," he said, friendly enough. "I come this way every day."

"Surely we've already gone further than that?"

"Well, I guess not," he said. He nodded, turned and descended again.

"I think I'm going to go back up," she replied, as if she owed him an explanation. "I'm late for an interview and..."

He'd already gone out of sight. She shrugged, turned, and started back up. After ten steps she stopped again, pulled off her too tight shoes with a sigh, then continued in just her tights.

As she climbed, she cursed the station announcer. Sure, he'd looked like he had a kind face, but he should have told her exactly how deep the stairs went.

Megan heard that wheezing breath again. A pair of worn brown leather shoes came into her eye-line, topped by dirty woollen socks and creased brown cords. He was siting on a step with a hankie pressed to his brow. He shook his head slightly as she approached.

"I'm beat," he said to her through heavy breaths but with a smile. "The doctors say I need the exercise, but this is too much for me. I just need to catch my breath."

"Yeah, I'm feeling that too." She welcomed the opportunity to rest her own legs and lungs as she waited a moment just down from him. The two shared an uncomfortable laugh.

Then they both glanced up the stairs, as the sound of heavy footsteps, then a pair of grubby boots, heaved down above them. A tall, heavy-set man with tired eyes and paint on his trousers was plodding down.

"Is everything okay?" he asked, glancing down at Megan, then the old man sitting on the step.

"Oh, fine," the man in the blazer replied. "We're just taking a moment."

Megan said, "It's a long staircase, but neither of us realised it was this long." She smiled. "I'm late, so I'm heading back up."

"Yeah, we must be pretty deep. I didn't know the Tube went this far down," replied the man standing above them.

"That's the thing," she said. "I've already been way further down. Then I came back up again. It must be five minutes since I turned around."

The three waited in uncomfortable silence. It was still a long way up from here, and Megan was definitely going to be late for that interview. But they'd understand about late Tube trains, wouldn't they? She should carry on up because every second she stood there was another one wasted.

They all laughed. Awkward.

She couldn't leave this man sitting here on concrete steps. If she was going up, she should offer to accompany him back to platform level and put him into the hands of the station announcer.

Can you give an example of when you've put someone else's needs above your own ambition?

Funny you should ask...

"Come on," she said to the man with the grey hair, trying to hide her resignation. "I'll take you back up with me. We'll go at your pace."

She held out her hand to steady him. He reached out to hold it, then suddenly pulled it back again as if remembering something.

"It's okay," he said. "Thanks. Just give me a few more seconds and we'll go up."

They waited again, and Megan looked up at the face of the

heavy-set man. He seemed to be wondering what his own next move was going to be. Then he raised his eyebrows and looked down over her shoulder. There was a sound of shuffling feet below them, then the puffing of breath. The young man in the suit came around the corner and up towards them.

"Are you the girl I just saw down there?" he asked. She bristled at being called a girl, but nodded.

"Well, since I saw you I walked about 100 steps. Still no bottom. Does anyone have any idea what's going on?"

Giles was lying. He'd done at least another 150 steps further down. Perhaps it was the hangover, but he'd begun to doubt himself. Maybe the staircase was 139 steps, or 149? By the time he'd stopped counting, the bright staircase lights and the dizziness of going round and round in circles were too much for his headache to handle.

You going crazy again, Giles?

He stopped to take another glug of Lucozade. He could feel his heart pounding in his chest, his ears ringing.

Forget work. He was really ill. It was going to be one of his bad days. Giles had decided to go back up, back onto the Central Line, back to Snaresbrook, back home and back to bed. Asswipe could put that in his special book and shove it up his rear.

It'd just be another day of boy's talk, anyway. Who's traded the most? How pissed they were last night? Which women they'd scored?

Then back to the pub for more. God, he had to get out of this job.

By the time Giles had expected to see the top of the staircase again, all that came into view was the woman he'd passed on the way down, the old guy who was now sitting on a step, and now another guy with broad shoulders who looked like he'd just stepped off a building site.

By unspoken consent, all four of them headed back up.

"You know," said the older man. "There are dozens of underground stations no longer in use. All with staircases, secret passageways."

"Shouldn't you be saving your breath for climbing," said Giles.

"Just saying, maybe we took a wrong turn. I've seen about it on TV. There's a whole warren of places just like this."

"Sounds about right to me, friend," said the builder.

Giles knew the old timer was right. It's easily done. Bank was famous for being complex. The way it joined with the Northern Line, but also at Monument and the Waterloo Line, and the Docklands Light Railway. On the Tube map, the changes looked simple. But you could walk half a mile underground right here, just to change lines. One wrong turn down the Tube station corridors and you could end up at the opposite end of where you wanted to be.

Giles edged between the girl and the older man, excusing himself as politely as his headache allowed. He tried to keep pace with the builder. The old chap was already wheezing again by the time he went past, and it wasn't long before he heard behind him the man's request to rest for a minute.

Giles put his head down and carried on.

"Okay," said the girl, obviously frustrated. "Listen, tell me your name. I'll go up ahead and send someone down to fetch you."

"It's Charles."

"Charles, it's not far away now, I promise you. But I think

you need help from someone who knows what they're doing. I'm just on my way to an interview."

"Thanks, I'll wait here for a minute, then carry on up. I'll be alright."

"Well, I'll send someone to meet you, anyway."

"Okay…?"

"It's Megan," she said.

"Okay, Megan. Thank you. You're a sweetheart. I shouldn't have come this way."

Dead right, thought Giles. What was the old guy even thinking? He barely looked liked he could stand, let alone handle steps.

Megan. *Sweetheart.* Nice name. Giles took a deep breath, pushing away thoughts.

The three continued up the stairs. Giles following the man in the big boots, followed by Megan and her feet covered only by sheer tights.

One. Two. Three. Four.

It wasn't long before Megan was lagging. Giles' head was pounding, and he felt like throwing up. He pulled the near empty bottle of Lucozade from his pocket.

27, 28, 29.

The guy in the boots just kept going. Bound to be strongest, what with working out on a building site. A free daily workout, basically. Not like Giles' Fitness First membership that he never even used. Free from work.

Three times a week. Up at six, in the gym for seven, in the office by eight. Beats the hangover every time.

Yeah, right? And how long since he'd played rugby? Despite his boarding school sports, free sports at every turn at Uni, lifetime membership of Cambridge Rowing Club, even a position on the squash ladder for a short time one Michaelmas term, Giles had done next to nothing for years to stay fit. All the opportunities barely taken advantage of.

The builder. He was fit on the job, not a bottle of energy drink in sight. He admired the guy. He was jealous, even.

Giles' breathing was heavy now, and his legs were beginning to ache. Megan had disappeared way behind.

79. 80. 81.

It took until Giles had counted to 129 again - Jesus, the second time on this staircase - for him to stop. He could still hear the boots above him, but could no longer see the guy who was wearing them.

"Hey, excuse me, something's not right here." The boots stopped, and Giles heard heavy breathing from the bloke for the first time. "We should definitely be back at the top by now. You didn't see a door or anything?"

"No mate, no door. Just more steps."

"There must have been a corridor we missed."

"I told you, no door."

Giles turned, sat where he was. He checked his watch. Twenty past nine. The other guy came back down to join him.

"I make it nearly half nine," Giles said. "I reckon I've been walking up and down these steps for fifteen minutes at least. Does that seem right to you?"

"Mate, I don't know. I don't know this way, never been on this staircase before. But I know I'm shattered. I've been shovelling hardcore all night."

He sat above Giles.

"Yeah, and I could do with a fag." Giles didn't want the guy to know how wrecked the staircase had made him. He was pleased the builder was now suffering too. "And a piss."

Giles definitely hadn't seen a door himself. In fact, he had seen nothing. No posters, no broken tiles. Just lights embedded in the roof every seven or eight steps, and the metal bannister rubbed smooth by so many hands over the years. As the stairs spiralled, everything looked the same.

He tried to think of yesterday. Coming down the same way. It was busier then. There had been no reason to look around, no reason to notice anything different. Just follow the head in front and keep going until you reach the platform. Same drill every day.

He pulled out his phone. Only half the battery left. He'd been playing one of those stupid games on the Tube earlier, that and listening to music. Until he'd given up because the school kids were making his head hurt.

"No signal," he said.

The bigger bloke didn't answer. Didn't even smile. Megan hauled herself up the stairs below them and looked up. Her face didn't register the slightest surprise to see them both. She'd obviously come to the same conclusion as they had. She sat on a step.

Giles shouted, "Hello, is anybody up there? Hello?"

Nothing.

"Sorry," he murmured to the others, a little embarrassed that he'd called out. Then he couldn't help himself.

"Hello!" even louder this time. He watched Megan flinch from them noise as it echoed up and down. Everyone held their breath, waiting to hear the faintest sound.

"Shit, what's going on?" the girl said, her voice slightly shrill.

"Hello?" she shouted. "Help us, we're stuck down here. Help us!"

Giles noticed she had started to shake. She was digging her fingernails into her palms, hunching her shoulders.

"Help us! Please, God, help us."

"It's okay," the builder said. "Listen, it's going to be okay. We're all here. We'll work it out together."

The girl settled.

Giles just sat there. He felt his headache ebbing away. It had been replaced by a sickening feeling that had nothing to do with last night's session.

4

Huffing and puffing, Charles eventually joined the three sitting on the steps of the spiral staircase. He pulled out his hankie again, wiped his brow. He used the solid bannister to lower himself onto a step.

All four were now sitting in silence. Looking at the surrounding walls, the staircase up and down.

"Hardly the Vatican is it," said Giles.

Only the older man laughed.

"Not quite," he said.

"Sorry?" said Megan, drying her tears.

"Vatican City Museum, you know in Rome," said Giles. "There's a huge spiral staircase there. I visited it once. The museum and the staircase. It was a while ago, now."

"Actually, there's two spiral staircases at the Vatican Museum," said Charles, ignoring the younger man as he tutted and rolled his eyes. "Possibly the most famous spiral staircases in the world. Each of them are also *actually* two staircases."

He turned to the others, a little excited. Maybe talking

might help keep the young woman distracted. Until they understood their situation.

"The original architect designed the two staircases to interweave, like a helix, though hundreds of years before DNA was observed," he motioned with his hands, attempting to show how the stairs wound around each other. "It's all granite columns and marble freezes. It doesn't actually have steps, it just slopes.

"But the other one, that was built less than 100 years ago. Same helix shape, but with steps. Over 130 of them, I think. But it gives you a weird feeling looking over the edge. It's an incredible sight. That one is open to tourists as part of the museum tour."

"You been there, then?" asked Giles.

"Many times. Of course, I was rather fitter then. And my wife Felicity was there with me."

Giles shook his head.

"That sounds lovely," said Megan. She smiled.

"Lovely compared to this?" asked Benny, obviously joking. Charles smiled back.

The group was silent again.

"It's ironic, really," said Charles, realising he'd distracted the group for a moment.

They all looked at him.

"Up there." Charles pointed to the ceiling. "I imagine almost exactly above us, or not far away..."

"Go on," said Benny.

"Well, it's Monument isn't it?"

"The Tube station?" asked Giles.

"*The Monument* itself. The immense column? It's one of the big London landmarks. At least in the City."

Gradually, each of the others nodded. Though Charles wasn't sure if they were picturing the same tower he was.

"In the centre of the crossroads, not far above us, is the column that marks the great fire of London."

"1666," Megan jumped in.

"Correct," said Charles.

She smiled. "Sorry, I remember little from my history. But that's firmly on any Londoner's history syllabus."

Charles was pleased with the attention, especially from Megan.

"Well, the Monument actually has a spiral staircase inside it. You can go all the way to the top. Over 200 feet, I think."

"That's pretty awesome," said Benny. "I mean, I work on some big buildings. But that must have taken some heavy brickwork."

"Christopher Wren designed and built it. It took six years. Completed in 1677.

"And here's the thing," said Charles. "It's really narrow," he indicated his surrounds. "The steps are concrete, and if I've got it right, there are 311 of them."

Benny whistled. "That's some climbing."

It was Megan's turn to point to the ceiling.

"So, it goes up above us, further than we've come down?"

"Probably," said Charles. "Two hundred feet is 65 metres."

Giles interrupted.

"Wait, are you saying this might be relevant? Has anyone ever been trapped on those staircases? Could we somehow be on that staircase, or something?"

Charles detected the panic again.

"No. Just thinking about similar staircases. Useful to know where we stand, I guess. Just passing the time."

"It is really interesting, Charles," said Megan. He smiled up at her. "How do you know so much?"

"History teacher," he said. "Well, I was. Anyway, you get to know these things. Like the Tube lines and the statues, and monuments and the museums.

"You don't look old enough for retirement," said Megan.

Charles smiled again.

"Well, they gave me no choice. Gardening leave." He hesitated. He wanted to tell them how unfairly he'd been treated. But now wasn't the time.

"I guess they wanted the new, younger teachers to come in. Things I've lived through are *taught* as history now. The Cuban Missile Crisis. September 11th. Iraq and Afghanistan. That Apple guy, and the Facebook kid.

"Time to move on, but I still like passing the time telling people what I know."

"Like I say, it's interesting to listen to," said Megan.

Charles nodded again.

The younger man spoke, rather curtly Charles thought: "Well, I'd rather pass the time looking for a way out of here, if you don't mind. Any ideas?"

Megan stood. If she would not get to the interview, she might as well show some of her newly learned management skills right now. All that new confidence she was determined to display, out of sight of Dad.

"So, what do we know? All inputs welcome. Bright ideas. Little clues. No wrong answers."

She knew she was pushing herself to say it, but it was this, or embarrass herself again by sobbing like a baby who's lost a toy.

The thin man in the suit shook his head.

"Anyone?"

"We're stuck down a spiral staircase, and I'm feeling wrecked," he said.

Megan stifled a little crossness.

"That's great, thank you...."

"It's Giles."

"Thank you Giles. While we're at it, why don't we introduce ourselves. So, Giles?"

"Do we have to do this?"

"Man, why are you being such a dick." It was the other, bigger man. "Answer the woman. At least she's doing something."

"Okay, sorry. Headache. I'm Giles. I work in the city. I was on my way to work, close to London Bridge. A big firm that's one of the top for financial trading in Europe, actually. And now, I'm super late and may well get sacked."

Work hard, play hard. Keep this country running, really. Another drink?

"Well, thank you again Giles," Megan tried hard not to say *for sharing.* She felt like a fool, but the stage was hers and it looked like the only opportunity she was going to get to perform today.

"And Charles, we know you've been a history teacher. Anything else to share?"

"I'm 60 and live alone. I was on my way to the British Library at Euston to do some research. I come in most days. Sad, really. Not very exciting."

"You always been a history teacher, Charles?" It was the builder who asked.

"Navy, prior to that. Another case of young ones coming in and booting out the oldies like me. I was only 30. Anyway, ended up teaching. Like most of us did. That or middle management in a bank."

Megan noticed how comfortable Charles seemed to be,

not only with his surroundings, but especially with the builder. She had always been a little hesitant with men. Thanks to Dad, probably.

But there was something else. Why wasn't Charles, well, why didn't he seem the slightest bit *hesitant* around the builder. Most white old people feared black men, didn't they? Hell, most white people of any age were afraid of black men. Especially those built as big as he was.

But Charles seemed entirely comfortable.

Silence.

The builder spoke.

"Well, I'm Benny. I work on building sites, and I've been shovelling materials all night. My back is killing me, my feet are sore in these boots. I was on my way home in Acton, where I was going to sleep until nightfall and do the whole thing over again. That's my life. That's all there is to tell."

"That's great Benny," said Megan. "I guess you know a bit about the structure of buildings, brickwork…"

"Tiles, concrete and that? Yeah, they teach you the basics. But I'm just a labourer. All muscle, not much up here." He tapped his temple.

"I'm sure that's not true," said Megan.

He smiled a little.

Silence.

"Oh, okay, my turn? I'm Megan, I live with my Dad in Epping, and I'm trying to get out of a crappy local secretarial job and into something in a legal firm in London. Today is my second interview. Sorry, *was* my second interview. So, it's back to my boring, go-nowhere job tomorrow.

"I enjoy dancing, and singing, and yoga, and hanging out with my friends, and music and watching TV. And I'm only joking about all of that. Except my job, which really is crappy."

All of them smiled.

"And now I'm down here with you guys, and I don't have a clue what to do next."

"You asked what we knew," said Giles. Megan was pleased that the guy was finally playing along. Offering a bit of camaraderie.

"I did," she answered.

"Well, we know we've walked down a very long spiral staircase," he said. "And I've always counted 129 steps on my commute. I think there's even a sign that says it at the top. But I know for a fact that I walked further than that from where Charles sat down."

"Okay," said Charles. "That's minus 129 plus from where we started. Who went further up then?"

Giles and Benny lifted their palms slightly.

"I walked 129 steps up from where Charles first sat down, and Benny did more," said Giles

"Another 20 maybe?" said Benny.

"Okay, call it 150 steps," said Giles. "Then you and Charles caught up with us, so that puts us, right now, at..."

Giles stopped for a moment.

"Two hundred and seventy-six steps below us, at least, and nothing at the bottom?" said Charles.

Megan cursed.

"But no one has gone any further up from here?" said Giles

"But we all came down, didn't we? Does that count?" said Benny.

"Of course it does," said Giles. "We came down, so there's a top."

"But we've already come up as far as the top should be," said Megan. "So, for the sake of keeping sane..."

"Sane?" said Giles. "I can't keep track of who's speaking, let alone the numbers."

"For the sake of our sanity, let's assume we didn't come down to here. Just for a moment, let's imagine that. Don't we just have to go up?"

Megan watched her fellow captives. Was that the right word? Commuters didn't seem right. Colleagues wasn't right either.

Each of them was probably feeling the same as her. Puzzled, annoyed, tired.

What they were probably not feeling, and what she'd kept from them with every ounce of her being right now, was her creeping feeling of claustrophobia. Megan didn't like tight, enclosed spaces. She never had.

Benny stood.

"You say the staircase should have been 129 steps?"

Giles nodded.

"I'll go up that far, and if I find anything, I'll send for reinforcements. Otherwise I'll come back down."

"And I'll go down 129 steps, if that's what we're working with. Just to make sure I wasn't just a turn from the platform." Giles smiled. "I may be some time."

5

Megan had been trapped in a dark black dustbin when she was younger. She couldn't remember how old she had been, but she must have been quite small to have even got in there. Seven, eight at most?

Dad didn't let her play with kids from school, but some of those who lived on her street he said were okay because he knew their parents. Those kids used to get together on summer evenings, and occasionally she'd persuade him to let her play too. They'd play until they couldn't see each other clearly any more. It wasn't that dark, but it was dark in the bin.

It was one of those black plastic bins you don't see much anymore. Before the ubiquitous great and green wheelie bins. They were completely black, had *Not for hot ashes* embossed on the lid. Megan always wondered what that meant: *Not for hot ashes.* The only time she'd heard the word ashes was something to do with Granny dying and her body being burned at a funeral. Did people fling dead bodies into the bins after the ceremony?

At the houses of most neighbours, the bins were hidden

from view by wooden trellis grown over by climbing plants or tucked behind small privet hedges. Her Dad would take out the rubbish from the kitchen and dump the bin liners into the black plastic tubs ready for collection.

The bins had been collected that morning, which meant the plastic bins were empty. And as usual, the refuse collectors hadn't bothered to put them back behind the bushes. Instead, two bins sat by the low brick wall at the front of Dad's house. One of them had its lid thrown to the floor.

Looking back, the bin men ought to have fixed that lid back on top of the bin. There were metal clasps at the top that could be pulled up to stop smells from escaping from the bin. To stop foxes and rats from getting in.

And to prevent little girls from climbing into a bin to hide on a balmy evening night when she and her friends were still out playing Forty-Forty and her neighbour Katie was leaning up against a big oak tree with her head buried in her arms counting to twenty before she'd come and look for them all.

Megan only had to wait until some of her friends had been found, or she'd heard someone shout Forty-Forty at the top of their voice when they touched the oak. They'd then be crowned winner of the game and counter next time.

Megan didn't want to win. It's no fun being the youngest and not being able to find people. Whenever she was 'it', the game lasted less than a minute before a laughing cry of Forty-Forty would be shouted and the rest would all climb out from their obvious hiding places - low down behind Dad's car, down the little valley that led to a stream, even behind the Forty-Forty tree itself - and they'd tease her about how bad she was at the game.

No. Megan didn't want to win. But she didn't want to be found either.

The bin seemed like a good enough place to hide. It was clean inside, and she could dip into it by wiggling over the side from the low wall, then pull the lid on top. She'd have to crouch, but the bin was wide enough to take her legs in a squatting position. She pulled on the top just as she heard Katie shout, 'coming, ready or not'.

Megan never found out who pulled the clasps over the lid. She just heard a clunk against the plastic. She heard a light giggle that could have been a girl or a boy. Then footsteps running away.

She pushed up at the lid with her head, but it wouldn't budge. She tried her arms, shifting them uncomfortably from her sides and heaving. But still no movement. It was only then she noticed how totally dark it was inside. Before it was just as if she'd closed her eyes tightly, a seven-year-old being brave in a game. But now she was really looking around, eyes wide open, and still couldn't see a thing.

The switch from feeling clever with her hiding place to absolute panic was immediate. She leant back against the inside of the bin and hammered with her fists on the lid. She stamped with her feet. She screamed. She wept in total and utter fear.

She elbowed the side, threw her whole body around, bruised her head as she banged it again and again and again.

She felt absolute mind-numbing terror so strong she couldn't even think about how it had happened, how stupid she had been, what she was going to do to get out, or even whether she'd suffocate. For Megan, it was already over. She kicked and screamed and punched and gulped air as if fighting away death itself. *Not for hot ashes.*

And then the lid came off. She heard tiny running footsteps go past again, but there was no giggle this time. She sprang from the bin, leaping onto the low brick wall and kicking the bin away from her with a thrashing of her feet. Her face was soaked with tears and she could hardly catch her breath. She sat on the wall, her back to the Forty-Forty oak, sobbing but trying to rub away the tears. Her friends would tease her for being a scaredy-cat. Don't show it.

Megan never found out who released her from the bin. Whoever it was, it was the same person who must have followed her as soon as Katie starting counting. They must have seen her climb in and then locked the lid over her head. It didn't matter, because she was out. She could breathe again.

When she turned back to the tree, the game had broken up and each of the kids was ambling quickly and silently back to their houses. No one said goodbye. A game gone too far.

She didn't tell. She'd be in big trouble for what she'd done and didn't want to face Dad.

There might have been some huge street palaver. She would be at the centre. Dad would be furious with her. Every neighbour was a customer, he would say. She'd ruin his business with her stupid behaviour.

But that night she begged Dad to leave the landing light on. To leave her bedroom door open just a few inches. She'd never been afraid of the dark before. She was always a little scared after.

Megan never played Forty-Forty again. And for the last eighteen years she had never gone to bed without at least a small orange glow nearby. Softening the darkness. Allowing her to sleep.

Megan looked around her. The curved walls around her felt closer than they had been. But surely that was an illusion. And anyway, to the front and the back, the space stretched endlessly. Wasn't that the problem?

Unusually, Megan felt herself wishing for six sides. Four on each side, as well as the ceiling and floor. Because at least one of those sides would contain a door, a window, a way out of here. A little normality.

The two younger men had gone off in either direction. Benny venturing still further up the steps, while Giles had gone down. Megan had suggested they all stick together until they were rescued. Giles thought that was silly. They didn't need to be rescued; they hadn't fallen down a mine shaft or got trapped under rubble. It was just a case of keeping going until one of them reached the end. Benny had shrugged his shoulders, remaining distant and thoughtful.

She'd stayed to look after Charles. His face had gone red, the colour wasn't abating, and he was gasping deeply.

Giles had - far too reluctantly, Megan felt - offered Charles the last swig of his Lucozade. What was Charles? Sixty did he say. And clearly not in the best of health. Giles was, despite his obvious hangover, relatively fit and certainly not as in need of an energy drink as Charles.

God, he was probably the guy who sat and pretended not to notice when obviously pregnant women stood next to him on the Tube.

Megan looked around the chamber more closely. Each step was about a foot and a half long at the thick end of the wedge, where it met the outside wall. The connection was seamless with the concrete of the step and its painted scuffed yellow edge leading into the dark tiles. At the thin end of the wedge, the step tapered into just an inch, where it met a solid concrete column, arranged in sections placed on top of each other.

The outside wall rose to about a metre, where the thick iron bannister was attached, then continued up to normal head height, before curving over at its highest point. Benny's head cleared it by a foot. Megan reckoned she could stand, reach her hands up and just about be able to place her palms against the curved ceiling. In line with the steps, the ceiling spiralled down with the stairs.

Along the highest point of the curve sat a row of lights embedded into the concrete. Each was about the size of the bottom of a coffee mug, and the row stretched forwards and backwards along the chamber, with one light every seven or eight steps.

The glass in the lights was dirty with grime, but no dirtier than the rest of the chamber. The steps had a gritty feeling, no doubt from dust and stones trodden down there by commuters passing this way. The tiles that surrounded the whole chamber were also coated in a thin film of dirt.

Charles coughed. A gravelly hack that sounded as if some of the grit and dirt had gone down his throat, and hadn't been washed away by Giles' drink.

"Are you okay Charles?" Megan asked.

He coughed again before answering. "Yes, yes. Just feeling a bit worn out. Should have brought some water. But I'm usually in the library by now with a cup of tea."

Megan looked at her watch. The four of them had been down here for over an hour now. That's if there were four of them left. Maybe Giles or Benny had made a break for freedom by now. She smiled. Some chance.

"Do you think they'll be long?" Charles asked. "Only, weak bladder and all that. Won't be long until I need to find a toilet."

Charles didn't seem to have a clue about their situation. He'd only walked a fraction of the steps up and down. To him, it was all still a minor confusion.

But he had a point. Megan now felt a little pressure from her own bladder. She didn't know what was harder: blotting out the creeping fear of being down here for days, or the now growing urgency of her need to pee.

Thanks a lot Charles.

When the others came back – she did already *know* they would come back – she'd have to continue to take charge. Giles seemed too flaky. Benny, well, just not bothered. Might as well use some more from that course on leadership she had taken.

That was the stuff she had planned to talk about at her interview, which now, she looked at her watch again, would have been well and truly over.

Just middle management guff her dad would have said. Far too many managers. Haven't got a clue. Never seen a day of work in their lives. Better roll up their sleeves and pick up a spade. Learn a proper trade. Country would be better off for it.

All the while he'd be shoving bank notes from his latest job into his back pocket. Let's keep that from the nosy bastards at the tax office, shall we? See these darlin' - he meant Megan - these hands? These are working hands.

She looked at her own now. They were grubby, with the dirt worked into the creases. She laughed as she thought about the hand cream she'd rubbed into them this morning. Dirty enough for you, Dad?

She shook her head. No, she'd have to resume charge. Allocate jobs. Someone to deal with toilets, someone to deal with food and water, someone to think about rescue, someone to think about passing the time in a dim tunnel without end, with nowhere to sleep or even properly sit down, with nothing to do but stare at the ever enclosing walls, until they all went completely, totally and utterly mad.

Who was she kidding? There were no toilets. She didn't have any food or water. Did anyone else? And rescue, from what?

None of this made sense. There had been nothing about this in her marketing and management course syllabus. There was nothing like this in any of her experiences. Nor Dad's. He'd not been down a mine. Hell, he'd never even been into a cave.

It wasn't like they were trapped down here. There was just no way out. Not the same thing.

But what Megan felt now, as she sat next to Charles, was exactly that. Just an inkling, just the tiniest seed of that same sensation of the bin when she was a kid. Of being totally and utterly trapped, surrounded by darkness. The meek little girl again, cruelly scared by someone playing a big joke.

She thought she had learned not to be that girl. She thought she was a strong, uncompromising, ambitious woman, despite the lack of support from her father.

But now, Megan felt that deep panic throw out fresh shoots into the pit of her stomach. They'd crawled outwards, down into her abdomen, up into her chest, stepping up her spine, vertebra by vertebra. She tried to ignore the feeling, struggling to push the creeping terror back down.

She was grateful to smell a faint whiff of cigarette smoke rising from below.

6

Giles held the cigarette in his mouth as he climbed the final few steps to where Megan and Charles were sitting. He took long drawn out puffs to calm his nerves and dissipate his laboured breathing.

He'd resisted so far. He wasn't a 20 a day man, just kept a pack of Camels on him for social situations - outside the pub on a sunny day with the boys from the office - and for stressful ones, like sitting at home alone half-drunk after another night out with them wondering where his life had gone.

This was one of those situations that demanded a cigarette. Giles had headed down the stairs again, walking as far as he could bear, until he felt the walls closing in on him. The incessant repetition of step after step; light after light; tile after tile was pressing in on his skull. He'd turned on his heels in frustration, even anger, and by the time he'd begun to retrace his steps he was ready for a fag.

He looked at his watch. It was now past 11 a.m., they'd been down here nearly two hours. Yes, this was officially one of those stressful situations. Underground regulations or not, he was lighting up.

Actually, good idea. He might set off a fire alarm somewhere. Right now he'd welcome a finger wagging official in a London Underground uniform coming to tell him off. He'd have a few things to say himself: like why don't you properly close off the old staircases.

He checked the pack, tapped one of the eight cigarettes out and lit it using the lighter he kept in the box.

As they came into view, Charles coughed from the cigarette smoke, first lightly then with more difficult breathing. Giles looked at Megan, almost challenging her to say something.

She raised her eyebrows.

Ah, look Giles, she desperately wants one too, you can tell. Not habitual. But easily persuaded to rekindle her teenage years.

She said nothing about the cigarette.

"So, I'm assuming it was the same deal?"

"No," Giles said. He took the Camel from his lips and blew the smoke at the ceiling. "The platform is down there. Along with rows and rows of tables stocked with food and booze and You've Been Framed are there to tell millions of viewers what mugs they've made of us."

"Okay, we need strategies," Megan said. Giles felt a light punch in the stomach that she'd ignored his joke. "Charles here needs to go to the toilet. I wouldn't mind myself, so I think we need to allocate a toilet area until we're rescued."

"Be my guest," Giles said, sweeping his hand down the stairs, with a grin on his face. "I've already relieved myself about 100 steps down, so might as well call that the toilet area. "Though, it looks as though Charles has already created one of his own."

They peered down at Charles' crotch, where a wide damp patch had appeared on the outside of his cords.

"Oh, oh dear, I'm sorry, I just couldn't control it," he said, a quiver in his voice. He pulled out a new handkerchief from his pocket and started dabbing away where the material of his trousers had turned dark.

"Do you want me to help you down there," Megan asked him.

"No, oh gosh no. I'm so embarrassed. I'm sorry, I'm such an old fool. Sorry," said Charles.

I like the sound of that, Giles. Maybe she'll help you down there, too.

Giles shook the thoughts away. This was a serious situation. And it was getting worse. At least he'd remembered his cigarettes. Giles shivered, then made like he was shrugging his shoulders.

"Don't worry mate, it's happened to us all." He flicked the cigarette butt down the steps and sat down. The three of them sat in silence for a few minutes.

"Well, I guess I can't put off the inevitable." Megan broke the stillness in a weak voice, using the bannister to pull herself up. "100 steps down, right?" Giles noticed she avoided making eye contact with him as she passed him.

She'd only just gone round the corner before the images flashed up.

Not the peeing itself, Giles, but you have to admit there's something about her dropping her knickers down there?

He tried to push out the image of her exposed white backside.

You gotta give it to her, Giles.

Fuck off with you. Giles stared down, stood, and looked around the chamber again, trying to shake thoughts from his aching head. He gripped the bannister.

He stilled the thoughts for a moment. Calmed his headache.

"So, what's your deal, Charlie Boy?" said Giles, trying to make his voice jovial for the first time with the old man. "Where were you off to today?"

"The British Library," said Charles. The handkerchief was resting over his lap, hiding the wet patch. "I'm doing research, just some historical stuff. I used to be a history teacher, but I've stopped that now. I started going for my interest, I thought I'd write a book or something. I've not really thought about it too much."

Giles looked around him.

"What kind of history? World Wars and stuff?" World War II was about the extent of his GCSEs. He knew how to blag essays.

Then Giles had done politics, economics and human geography at A-level, with general studies, though even he didn't call that a real A-level. Then it was human, social and political sciences at Cambridge, just like everyone who worked in this crummy City.

"No, much older," Charles said. "Seventeenth century stuff. Trade links between the UK and all over Africa. British protectorates, Barbados, the Caribbean, shipping routes."

Giles definitely wasn't interested anymore. "Jamaica, and all that?"

"Well, not really, but..."

Giles welcomed the unmistakable clump of Benny's boots from above their heads, followed by the steel-toed boots themselves, and then the stout figure of the man walking in them.

As he came down, he was banging the tiles with a softly clenched fist and testing grouting with his fingernails, looking for a crack or something loose. Not looking for a way out, thought Giles, just trying to establish what we're really up against.

That's how this spiral staircase was feeling like. A battle.

"Where's Megan?" he asked, his voice sounding dry and tired. Giles felt like Benny wasn't surprised to see him.

"Our newly appointed luxury lavatory," said Giles. "All mod cons, just 100 steps down."

He never sounded as funny when he didn't have a pint in his hand.

———

Megan returned, and Giles spotted her taking a deep breath as she rounded the corner. As if she was steeling herself. Putting back on a different persona.

"Okay," she said, smiling up at Benny. "So, we've got a toilet and we now know Giles has cigarettes. What we really need is water and food, just in case. So, what have we got? Should we turn our pockets out?"

"Who put you in charge?" said Giles.

"Bah, just shut up man, my head hurts from your talk." It was Benny.

Giles was amused, only slightly offended. If the builder thought Giles was chattery right now, he just had to wait.

The builder just looked tired. Grateful to be sitting on the step again. In fact, Giles thought, he didn't seem to be worried by this entire episode. All that tapping on the tiles and running his fingers along the walls. He showed none of the creeping claustrophobia Giles was feeling. The same that he could see behind Megan's fake determined eyes.

Charlie? Well, he looked resigned to the situation, too. But not hemmed in.

Charles turned out his jacket pockets and placed them

on the step beside him. An A6 sized leather notebook, a blunt pencil, his wallet, a glasses container for his spectacles - now removed.

"No food. I usually take it at the library," he said.

Megan fished into her tiny handbag. It was an accessory for the now-defunct interview. Her Tube pass, a little makeup, a neatly folded CV she was taking to Rank and Tudor, a biro, a purse fat with coffee loyalty cards and her phone.

"Less than half charged," she said, putting it down. "No reception, obviously."

Benny fished into the deep pockets of his builder's trousers. He brought out a thick leather pouch with a zip, a wallet, a pencil, and then held up his mobile.

"Next to no charge," he added.

Giles laid his stuff on a step, too. Often he'd carry a man-bag to work, but he'd left it in the office last night, planning to collect it after he'd been for a few drinks. But it hadn't worked out like that. It hadn't worked out like that at all.

His now empty bottle of Lucozade. A pocket full of loose change, his wallet and mobile - next to no charge. He patted his inside jacket pocket, felt something inside, hesitated for a moment, then found his brushed-chrome roller ball pen. He put it on the step.

"So, we're all good for writing our last will and testaments with all the pens and Charles' pad," he said. The group smiled, but no one laughed. Charles pulled his note-book closer to him.

Giles added his cigarettes, "seven left".

Giles had left a few things out. He barely knew these people. It had only been a couple of hours. He suspected everyone else had left something out, too.

Megan looked down at the paltry stash. "So, we've got no

water or drink. And we've no food at all? And practically no mobile phone power between us?"

"Not that it would be any use," said Giles. "No one has a signal."

"We might need them for other reasons," she said.

"Tetris? Candy Crush?" Giles said. No laugh again.

Scanning through your pictures, Giles. There's some entertainment right there.

"Anything else?" ,

Giles felt her last question was asked with a deep quiver in Megan's voice.

She's cracking, Giles. Just a matter of time.

They all looked down at what they'd got. Megan turned away and stared at the floor between her legs. Giles knew she was weeping. He swore at himself for pushing her.

And for not bringing water. I mean, that was basic. Lucozade, for God's sake. After a night like last night?

Weren't the Tube posters always going on about taking a bottle of water with you when you travelled? All of them should have had a bottle of water.

The thought was almost impossible to contemplate. They had nothing to drink. Nothing to eat. They could be down here for days until they were rescued.

Giles swallowed deeply and felt only a smoky dryness pass down his throat. Maybe that fag wasn't such a good idea. How long was it that someone could survive without food and water? Five days? Three? The silence told him the others were thinking along the same lines.

You could always drink your own piss, ha ha ha.

Benny stood up and for a second Giles imagined the big man was going to take the Lucozade bottle and piss in it. But it was just his warped and hungover mind playing tricks on him. Benny headed down the stairs.

"100 steps for number ones," he said. "One hundred and fifty for number twos." He disappeared around the steps below them.

"Jesus, we'll all be super fit by the time this is all over," Giles said, trying to show a smile.

Charles breathed out heavily.

7
_____

Nilam Dewan only worked evenings. Between 3 p.m. and midnight at the Monco fuel station off the Wanstead Road in East London. The rest of the time, well, he was catching up on sleep or trying to put in time at the English language college he'd come from Sri Lanka to study at.

The Central London School of English Language had looked grand on the internet. The site had said it was on a quiet historic street off the Capital's famous bustling Oxford Street. What Nilam had found wasn't as advertised.

The Central London School of English Language was found in an alleyway between a mobile phone cover retailer and a computer repair store. There was a glass door, where other shops dumped their rubbish.

The door led to some stairs, and at the top of those were two tiny rooms with white boards at one end and a kettle at another. The pupils there - most as disappointed as Nilam to find themselves in less salubrious surround-ings than they'd hoped for - had to choose between the faint smell of damp with the windows closed, or the smell of trash and the noise of the traffic rising from the roads below.

But he was here now. He had to keep paying his class fees, and he needed somewhere to live. So he tried to attend class during the day, work late into the evening and to sleep in the student-packed shared house he'd found.

The later part of the evenings were always quiet at the fuel station. Parents had long been and gone for the after-noon school pickup, where they'd often call in for fuel on their way home or to swimming lessons or play dates. Most of the sales reps would refuel during the day, then they'd sit in the car park behind the station chomping on pasties and cups of insipid coffee from the machine. Commuters always filled up in the mornings, taking a brief break from the relentless traffic heading West and into the city.

By late evening, most had their evening meals and were settling in for the night. Those that were out to pubs and restaurants didn't drive these days, now that police conspic-uously rolled their squad cars up and down the Wanstead Road to kill time.

Taxi drivers. That was more or less the total of Nilam's trade once it had gone past 10 p.m. Most often those heading back into the suburbs after a busy day shifting City folk from tower to tower in the financial district. Though of course, he got a trickle of other cars pulling in for fuel, for a coffee or on a desperate search for milk, a loaf of bread or something overpriced and tasteless from the Monco's ready meal section.

The thin, waxy haired guy in an ill-fitting bomber jacket seemed unimpressed with the selection. He'd been browsing for five minutes, picking up punnets of mashed potato and microwave pork sausages, looking at the labels on lasagnes. He'll probably go for a burger in the end, with a grab-bag of crisps. He certainly looked like he could do with some fat on him.

The guy had either parked round the back or come on foot. Nilam hadn't had to click the screen to allow a pump to dispense fuel and could see his car wasn't parked round the front of the shop. It was close to 11 p.m., the time when Nilam would close the main doors and only serve customers through a serving hatch by the tills. Once this guy had got his food, that's what he'd do.

The door dinged and Nilam watched as two other customers entered the petrol station, one fat and wearing a cap, the other bulky and nervous looking, wearing a woollen hat. But they were both far from as indecisive as the burger man. They strode straight up to Nilam as he waited behind the till, and for a moment, both stared at him.

Hats. In a petrol station, hats were not good. Two hats were worse. Just in time - just in time to see the burger man turn and stride towards the front desk too - Nilam clocked that two hats plus a bomber jacket were even worse. He felt under the desk as the smaller man began leaning over the confectionary in front of him, shouting in his face.

"Get your hands from under the fucking shelf," the man in a cap said. The man in the bomber jacket had left the ready meals far behind and pulled out a sawn-off shotgun.

"Nice and easy, fella," not quite shouting, but pointing the gun between Nilam's eyes to make himself clear, "hand over the cash. Everything, empty the fucking till."

"NOW!" shouted the bomber jacket, flinging a black holdall at Nilam. The muscle man was now holding up a pistol, too. He was also pointing it at him. He was glancing at the forecourt every now and again, in case someone else came to fill up.

Nilam was stunned, instinctively holding up his hands.

This wasn't what he'd come from Columbo for. To be shot over the chocolate bars for the sake of an evening's worth of petrol station takings.

"Fill the bag," said one thug. Nilam couldn't help an internal smile as he looked down at the bag, though he ensured he kept a terrified look on his face.

What were these guys hoping for? This wasn't a bank, and any big notes went straight down the metallic security chute that Nilam didn't have a key to. Group 4 had cleared the shoot just before his shift started. Most paid by card anyway. What did the till contain? A couple of hundred quid?

Part of his training when he started at Monco was that Nilam should simply do exactly as he was told in these situations. Do it slowly, no jerky movements. Monco could stomach loosing a couple of hundred pounds, but it couldn't face losing an employee. Nilam had also learned about hidden CCTV, letting the robbers go and not trying to be a hero.

And the panic button under the till.

He moved slowly, keeping his right hand in the air and using his left to punch a no-sale code into the till, and pinged the drawer open. He noticed the white guy in the cap look into the drawer with a look of disappointment, quickly replaced by resolution.

"Hand it all over," he screamed at Nilam, who pulled out a handful of £20s and £10s, a couple of fivers, then stuck them in the black holdall where they looked embarrassingly small. The guy looked over at his accomplices.

"And the coins," said the black man, nudging the end of his gun in the till's direction. "Throw the coins in too."

Nilam dropped his right arm, again moving as slowly as he could, and with both hands scooped up pound coins and fifties in his fists, dropping them into the holdall. For a second he thought they'd might ask him to go for a handful of 20p coins too, even the coppers.

"Now, drop to the fucking ground," said the burger man. "Don't fucking move until we're out of here."

Nilam fell to his knees, but couldn't help notice one guy grab a handful of Snickers bars and a packet of crisps, throwing them into the bag too. By the time he was lying flat on the shop floor, he was almost giggling. He heard the three run from the shop, and the door dinged as they left. Still, he kept his head to the ground with his arms flat out in front of him.

He thought of the Sri Lankan civil war and how the last four minutes had been far from the first time he'd seen angry men waving guns. These guys were nothing compared with brutal paramilitaries, nor the Sri Lankan government troops when provoked.

He heard a car behind the garage screech out onto the road, and just in the distance the jumbled up sound of two police sirens ringing out. The button he'd pressed right at the beginning of the attack had summoned them.

He heard the Doppler-shift change in one of the sirens as it sped past the petrol station, while another came closer and he heard the police car as it skidded up within metres of the shop.

8

Giles' smoking didn't actually bother Charles. He used to be a big smoker himself, but gave up when he left the forces. It wasn't his lungs that was the problem. It was his heart.

The one thing Charles hadn't turned out onto the step was a small canister of heart pills. Statins, the doctor had called them. A low dose to be used when he felt twinges in his chest. He already knew he was the weakest link in the group, and they did too. But he didn't want them to know just how weak he was.

He'd been having painful twinges in his chest for the last few years. Felicity had nagged him about it, but only when they'd come more regularly had Charles bothered the doctor. The GP had done all the checks: stethoscope, ECG, bloods, asked Charles intrusive questions about his diet, his drinking, what exercise he took.

Doctor Stubbs had scribbled a prescription and handed it over. Just some heavy duty aspirin to take regularly.

"Take these," the doctor pointed to the scribbled word

simvastatin on the form, "any time the pain gets bad. Just to calm things down a little."

"Only one at a time, though," he warned. "We don't want to calm things down too much." Doctor Stubbs had smiled as he shook Charles' hand and led him back out to the waiting room.

Felicity had insisted Charles kept a plastic canister of the statins in his jacket pocket because he wore it almost every day. But in more recent months, he was forgetting to pack his pills. Sometimes forgot to take the aspirin too.

Felicity was what Charles called a 'good woman'. She'd worked as a typist for a local conveyancing firm pretty much since the kids had grown up. Just to fill the day, really. And when the company had modernised and Felicity found herself a little out of date, well, she happily walked away, living off their savings and Charles' teacher's salary. She found little groups to join, odd bits of charity and committee work.

When the doctor gave Charles his pills, she drew up a little exercise plan for him. She kept a record of his medication. She would have his aspirin on a little saucer each morning, next to his round of brown toast and a cup of tea - not too strong. She'd kiss him on the way out, check his cannister of statins, then head for one of her meetings.

In fact, she said she was busier than when she had the job. She certainly seemed happier than at the solicitors'. Her Soroptimist meetings, her house plants, the village committees. She was an 'upstanding member of local society' Charles would joke. She had a Queen-like sense of duty, the need to set a good example.

She was a great cook, too. Always baking, fussing over cookies for this fete or that. Every month she'd have an 'at home' with a group of other women from her various social circles. She'd spend days before, cleaning and preening, cooking and setting the dining room table. The one they only used on special occasions. When the kids used to come home for a big family Christmas.

Most days she'd have a meal on the kitchen table for when he got home. Or at least in the oven if she was out at the village hall. She looked after him and always asked him about how school had gone. How his pupils were getting on.

She'd even asked him how his out-of-school research project was going. She called it his hobby, but she meant it affectionately. The European expansion into Latin America and Africa in the 17th century wasn't everyone's cup of tea. But nor was flower arranging, sifting through donated junk or village litter picks.

Felicity knew that.

Obviously, she didn't know what the pupils said about him at school. And he never had time to explain.

Word gets around a small village like theirs. Particularly when your wife goes to every class, committee and council shindig in the Parish.

Felicity left within a week. Not a word of disapproval or upset. She just disappeared while he was out at the library. One bag was missing from the cupboard, along with a handful of dresses. Her house keys were sitting there on the kitchen table. His dinner was warming in the oven. A single bed time statin was waiting on his dinner plate.

9

"Noise," said Benny.

The three others looked up at him.

"Sound," he said. "Travels way faster than us, and way further."

"What you getting at?" said Giles.

"We need to send a sound. Up and down the staircase."

"Dead right," said Giles. He took off his shoes, slipped his hands into them, and weakly began beating the walls.

Bang, bang, bang.

"Help, help," he shouted. "Come on, you lot."

Benny took a moment to unlace his steel toe capped boots. Megan took her shoes from where they lay on the step.

"Is anyone there?" she shouted.

All three of them banged their shoes around the tiles, the steps.

"Wait," said Benny. "The rail."

The three began pounding the iron rail with their shoes, Giles and Megan shouting out for help. The frantic hammering of the rail formed itself into a rhythm.

Bash-bash-bash.

Bash-bash-bash.

Then quiet, while they listened to only a slight echo up and down the chamber, the listening for any response.

Bash-bash-bash.

Bash-bash-bash.

Charles just shook his head.

"What, Charles?" said Giles. "It's not like you're doing anything."

They all stopped banging and shouting for a moment.

"It's like this," Charles said. He tapped his knees with both hands.

Slap-slap-slap, (pause) slap (pause) slap (pause) slap (pause), slap-slap-slap.

"S.O.S?" said Giles.

Megan smiled.

"You're a genius Charles."

All four began in earnest this time. Smacking the soles of their shoes against the rail in an S.O.S. rhythm.

The sound was loud, but it didn't resonate very far up or down the rail.

After three minutes, they'd all given up.

"We should do it every hour, for five minutes at a time," Charles said. "That's what I was trained to do, at least. It's supposed to make it more noticeable from other noises."

"Every hour? I don't intend to be down here for many more minutes. This is crazy," said Giles. He paced up and down the few steps that surrounded him, patting the walls, pulling at the metal rail.

Benny looked closely at the man who'd just spoken. His hands were jittery. Could he see the odd twitch in Giles' neck?

Something wasn't quite right. And Benny had a good idea what it was.

Slowly, Giles calmed and sat down. Except for Megan, they put their shoes back on. Charles pulled out his notebook and made notes.

"What's in the notebook, Charlie Boy?" Giles called down to the grey-haired man.

"Don't call him that," said Megan. "It's Charles, isn't it?"

"It's okay," said the man below her. "I've been called much worse. They called me Charlie Boy in the Navy actually, that and other stuff."

"Is that what the book you're writing is about Charles? A memoir?" said Megan.

"Oh, gosh no. I've nothing in my life to be proud of. No, it's just notes, you know, my little interests. It's my private work. It's all I have, really."

"But you are writing a book?"

"Aren't we all?" he asked.

Megan smiled.

"It's about the 17th century trade routes. British Colonies, the Portuguese. Just technical stuff. I like the names of the ships. The captains. The big routes. When you're my age, you can only look back. I like to look back a long time."

"All very well, Charlie Boy," said Giles. "Tell us about the Navy. I bet you saw some action."

Everyone knew what Giles was implying.

Charles sighed.

"I was an in-betweener, really," he said. "Too young to serve in the Second World War. So I just sat around in the sea, going this way or that, not quite knowing why we were out there. When all the high technology came in, the nukes, the cold war, I was turfed out for the new kids. Got into teaching."

"I reckon you were a great history teacher," said Megan.

Charles shook his head and sighed.

"Anyway, looks like you're pretty comfortable down here." It was Benny who spoke this time. "First thing I noticed about you once this got real. No panic. You don't mind being deep? Small spaces?"

"Submarines," Charles said simply.

"I knew it," said Benny. "Tell me about small spaces. I can see it written all over your face. Hell, you almost look comfortable."

"Three months at sea at a time. Swapping bunks. Living under each other's feet. That's what fascinates me about the trade links way back then. How did they get so many…" he looked up at Benny, hesitated, "goods on board those ships. How those journeys changed the world."

Benny looked puzzled for a second. Then he got the implication.

"Ah, got you Charles," he said. "Slaves."

"It's just an interest. History. I promise you."

"It's cool, man," said Benny. "I'm from Hackney. My mum too, though originally from Nigeria. We all got a lot to learn about the past. Me especially. Don't know what my ancients did for me all those years ago. I haven't paid them back, neither. But I'm trying Charles. I'm trying."

"Fascinating," said Giles. Benny picked up the sarcasm.

"Oh, yeah? What's your story, white boy?"

"Nothing, sorry."

"Ah, well, you shut up or put up when this old man is telling his story. He knows more than any of us. Probably seen shit you and I ain't never dreamed about. You got to learn to respect your elders."

Megan spoke up: "Go on, Charles."

"We went all over the world in those subs. Africa, the

Caribbean, Latin America. The Pacific. All below the radar. Then Russia and China. Secret missions. Met all kinds of folk. Some guys down in the subs with me were from Lagos. They had a right to serve after the war. Good men, all of them."

He looked up at Benny. He smiled in return.

"So, I guess I know some useful stuff. From history, and from the services. Rationing. Being cold. Getting along when your shipmates are being *difficult*. Obeying orders."

There was a moment of silence. A few smiles.

"When to fight," Charles said, more seriously. "And when to give up."

Charles shook his head and stared at the ground.

"Taking your punishment," he said.

"Man, do I know that," said Benny. "These hard walls will give you that feeling any day of the week."

10

The S.O.S. banging continued on the hour, every hour, for the next three hours. Each time, the group replaced their shoes, shook their heads, and continued to wait.

At least it gave them structure, thought Megan. A marking of time passing. Soon, though, it would be past what they might normally call bed time. Would they carry on with the S.O.S. through the night?

Night. At least there was light here. Outside, it was dark by now. She thought of her bedroom at her Dad's house, miles away from here. Her bedside lamp would be on. She'd be curled up in her pyjamas. Comfortable. Safe.

Charles had fallen asleep. He was still wheezing. He'd taken off his blazer, wrapped it up into a ball, and was sitting against the wall. His head lolled forward onto his chest.

He still smelled from earlier. Or maybe it was just the stench from the toilet area rising. How long had it been? 11 hours? Megan looked at her phone. It had been 14 hours since she'd started down the spiral and she felt like she didn't know up from down any more.

She tried to swallow, but her throat was so dry. The only thing she could feel was the cold floor she sat on, and the pins and needles running up her spine and down the backs of her legs. All she could smell was what wafted up from what they'd all had to do a hundred steps down. She wished Giles would light up to mask the stench.

Were they even sitting near the surface? If they were 50 metres down, the rescue team could probably drill down. You'd see that kind of thing on the news every now and again.

Weren't those Chilean miners under for 40 days? Megan shuddered. She couldn't stand another hour in this place, let alone 40 days. She tried to remember the news footage. Those miners were getting food sent down to them through a tube. Her stomach ached.

Would rescue teams even be able to get to them? Maybe they were a couple of hundred metres down. Would they be able to dig that deep at all? Did anyone even know they were missing?

After the interview this morning, she'd planned to go for lunch by herself, then recover with a glass of wine in front of the TV. She'd send a few texts to say how it had gone. But she would not answer the phone. Didn't want to pull the interview apart and speculate.

That meant only Dad would miss her tonight. Probably only when he sat down to watch *The Apprentice* once he got back from the pub and noticed she was missing. He wouldn't ask about the interview. He'd fall asleep with a can of beer, assuming he'd forgotten some appointment she'd had.

Even tomorrow, the guys at work would only wonder why she hadn't come in today. They'd just get her answerphone when they called. It's not like they'd send out a search party or call 999.

And even if they did, the emergency services would not start drilling holes in London streets on the off chance she might be buried far down below.

Buried alive. She felt sick with the idea. Deep terrifying memories from being trapped in the bin welled upside her like bile.

I've got to get out of here. I'm going to die down a big hole and no one's ever going to find me. We can't just sit here. There has to be something we've missed. We've got to do something before we die.

She felt her cheeks burning up and her stomach retch. But there was no longer anything down there to come up. She struggled with the urge to spring up and holler and shout and bang her fists on the wall. To kick out.

The bin. She felt panic creeping up from her stomach again, threatening to release a scream, to let her body go into wave after wave of terror as she had done all those years ago. Megan crunched her fingers so tightly into a fist, she felt her nails cutting into her palms. The pain felt good. It calmed her.

She was determined that would not happen here. She may still need sleep with a chink of light always visible, but she'd learned to control her emotions. Knowing they were merely imagined physical urges.

She took some deep breaths, pushed the sickening feeling away, and tried to stare down the stairs in front of her.

Charles. She wished she could curl over and sleep like him. She felt a mix of jealousy and anger that he'd managed to drift off. She'd love to just close her eyes and shut the nightmare out. The dim light of the staircase could lull her to sleep. Then, she'd wake up again fresh. In her bed at home with her interview still before her. She'd definitely go for one of the old skirts this time. Take the bus and get there an hour early. If only she'd been less fussy this morning.

"I'm never using the Tube again in my life," she said out loud.

Benny smiled and shook his head.

"You might not get a chance," said Giles with an awkward smile. She felt her cheeks burn up again.

"Jesus, will you just shut up," said Benny.

Then the lights went out.

———

"Oh God, oh God," Megan began screaming. "Oh God, not this."

Her sobs echoed around the chamber. They bounced off the wall. Giles heard her kicking the walls with the soles of her shoes, sending a dull echo up and down the staircase.

Giles looked up around him. Nothing. He could see nothing. He waved his hands in front of his face. He closed his eyes and opened them. There was no difference. It wasn't just dark. It was pitch black. A darkness he'd never experienced before. Not the tiniest bit of light anywhere.

And now Megan was screaming, etching the sound like a weevil into his brain. He knew their problems had just got a thousand times worse.

"Calm down, Megan. Calm down." It was Benny, speaking in a soothing voice.

"I can't, we're going to die here. Oh, God. I can't see anything." She was blubbering now. He heard her hammering on the floor with her feet and hands. "We need help. We need help."

A green glow appeared behind Giles. Then an orange light waved around the staircase. Benny had turned on his phone torch and was looking around. It hovered on Megan. Giles saw she was rocking on her step, grasping her hands together and into her chest, as if they were a reassuring toy she needed to grasp close.

"Megan, take a breath." She looked up at Benny, and Giles saw the orange light reflected in her eyes. They were puffed up and streaming with tears. She started taking deeper breaths.

The light turned away from Megan and onto Charles. He was awake now, and blinking into the torch, a look of puzzlement on his face. A look that quickly turned to fear as he realised what was happening.

He mumbled, reaching for his glasses. As if that would do any good. He coughed. "Hello?"

"It's okay, Charles, we're all still here," said Benny. "We just lost the lights."

The glow spun around as he shone the light up the steps and Giles looked in the direction it was pointed. Then as the light swung back round towards him, he saw momentarily the spooky face of Benny in the glow. Giles did a double take, as if he'd seen a ghost.

Benny turned the light again, this time pointing it to the ceiling. It reflected a dim orange hue off the roof and walls, and back down onto Megan and Charles.

Giles reached into his pocket and pulled out his own phone, touched the screen and the orange-white light reflected onto his own face. He was looking for the button which would turn on his torch.

"What you doing, man?" Benny said.

"Same as you, giving us some light."

"Turn it off." Giles could hear the anger in Benny's voice.

"I've barely any battery left on mine. If yours goes too, we'll have nothing."

Megan spoke through her sobbing, "Mine went hours ago."

"Exactly," said Benny.

"It's my fucking phone," said Giles. "I'm about a quarter charged." Still, he let the phone screen grey out, go darker still before it returned to nothing.

"Okay, we need to think about this," said Benny. "Megan, Charles - can you hold on to something. The bannister?"

Charles went into a coughing fit, but said "okay".

"The bannister?" asked Megan.

"Megan, I'm going to turn this torch off."

"No, don't please." Giles watched her cry again, rocking forwards and backwards, digging her bruised tight fists into her chest.

"Megan, I need to turn this light off. We need the batteries. Hold on to something and we can talk in the dark, decide what to do."

She nodded weakly, then with a little more force.

"Okay, Benny," she said.

The torch went out, the green light of Benny's screen faded. Back to sheer blackness.

All Giles could hear was those two snivelling, then the even breath of Benny behind him.

"Right, brainbox," he said, turning his head and projecting his voice toward Benny. "Exactly what is it we're going to do?"

Why's he throwing his weight around suddenly, anyway? Okay, Benny was built for it but clearly couldn't match his brawn with his brains. Otherwise, why's he working on a building site?

The bloke's a grunt, pure and simple. Someone who could

haul sacks of broken bricks around, but only when someone told him to. Hell, Giles, you earn more than everyone else down here put together.

As quietly as he could, he reached around and found the bannister himself. He pulled on it, bracing its solidity, and shook his head to get rid of the chatter in his brain.

There was something about Benny. He'd hardly said a word since this whole thing started. Why didn't he talk, for God's sake? He just sat there, staring into space. He didn't even give the impression he wanted to get out of this.

Give him a line of coke, that'd spruce him up a bit. Put some wind in his sails. And that girl could do with something too. Lighten her up a bit too.

Giles closed his eyelids tightly, trying to shut out the thoughts. But open or closed, it wasn't getting any brighter down here.

"I have an idea," it was Charles, speaking through the darkness in almost a whisper, muffled by occasional sniffs. "I learned it in the Navy, in case the sub went dark. You see, the darkness benefits us."

"Oh, Charlie Boy. Nice of you to wake up and join us. Had a pleasant sleep?" said Giles.

"You're such a twat," said Megan.

Giles was taken aback by the sudden aggression from Megan. She'd been so prim and proper until now.

"Okay, Charlie Boy! How! How on earth could this *possibly* be a good thing?" The question was addressed to Charles, but the sarcastic tone was meant for Megan.

"Well, don't you see?" Charles' voice was clearer now, as if he'd pulled himself from his lying position and was sitting up on his step.

"No, we don't see," said Giles, listening out for a laugh which didn't come.

Charles continued: "The darkness means if we see any light at all, even the slightest chink, well, it would show there was a light somewhere. Out there. A way out. The outline of a door. A brick loose. Even a hole or a crack would give us something to start with.

"First rule on a sub. Don't panic, look for your nearest exit. Where is water leaking in? Where is air pressure being lost? Those are your ways out."

He had a point. Maybe they were all missing something. Maybe Giles could go 200 steps up and it would get lighter up there. Light can't go round corners, so it was possible if they continued up. Giles remembered how far they'd already gone. But maybe just a few steps more?

Everyone sat in silence.

"I'll go up," said Benny. There was no excitement in his voice. Just flatness. "I'll see if I can see anything. I'll go up 200 steps, no more, then come back down."

Charles said, "You'll need to go up in the dark. So you miss nothing."

"Yes, I'll go up in the dark. Giles, you've still got your phone if anything changes here." He seemed to pause. "Giles, look after these two."

Giles felt patronised, but grateful that he didn't have to climb any more steps. Was there just a little pride at being left to protect the rest? Real responsibility for a man like Giles?

"Okay, 200 steps," said Benny. "Ten minutes up max maybe, ten minutes down."

"Hey, make sure you count the steps down again," Giles said. "Otherwise, you might kick me in the face."

This time Megan sniggered, and Giles saw the joke. He had been harsh just now. Then they all shared a little laugh.

A slight feeling of unity as one of their members headed off into the abyss.

Giles heard a deep sigh from behind him, then the slow clump of Benny's boots as he headed into the darkness above, the sound of his hand edging along the bannister and pulling him up. Within a minute, there was silence again.

Giles was uncomfortable now. He didn't want to admit he appreciated the big man's presence, but now he was gone? Well, maybe he did prefer him around.

The adrenaline of being suddenly plunged into dark ebbed away, replaced only by the deep oppressive endless black all around. It was all he could do not to turn on his light. But he knew that wouldn't be any use and would probably shine up to Benny above. He cringed to the bannister more tightly.

"Just us then," he said to no one in particular, to break the silence. But Charles and Megan didn't reply, both obviously struggling to contain the same sense of helplessness and fear.

She's alright that Megan. Okay, a bit power suit and ambitious, but you couldn't really fault her for that. Wasn't that exactly how he'd been a year ago? And look where that got him: paid more, but hanging round with those idiots all day (and compulsory after-hours).

He wished he'd stayed where he was in sales. At least he'd get home on time, could sit on the sofa, watch the football (God, even a detective series or something), eat a TV dinner instead of those tiny plates of tapas they served in *La Cascada* opposite the office. Food that left you so hungry you were bound to get a kebab later on.

The thought of a kebab made his stomach rumble, but in his throat he felt sick. How could he eat that pile of gristle and offcuts, all that onion and chilli sauce? And what on earth made him think that picture - that breath afterwards - would be attractive?

Women went for him sometimes, he reminded himself. And when they didn't, well when you've got the money anything can be bought. That's the mantra of financial trading.

That Meg is a seven or eight at least. Go on, Giles, admit you would. Nice tight arse, out here, in that blouse.

He imagined the hand gestures they'd make in the pub.

Yeah, I'd have a crack if I were you. Another pint of Dutch courage, then take her over a drink. If you don't, I will.

Giles felt a brief stirring.

"Alright, just to change the atmosphere here," he said into the darkness. "You got a boyfriend Megan?" He noticed too late that he hadn't bothered to ask Charles about his love life.

"Not that it's any of your business, but no," she said. Giles felt the stirring solidify. He put his hand down, just to re-arrange things.

"Had one lately? You know, got anyone on the go at the moment? Good-looking girl, climbing the career ladder. I reckon you'd be quite a catch."

"No one significant."

Giles thought he heard the tentativeness in her voice, as if she was trying not to give too much away. Not to commit.

Go on, that's an entry pass, isn't it. Playing it coy.

A croaky voice came out of the darkness: "I had a wife," said Charles. "Felicity. But she's gone now."

"Oh, I am sorry," said Megan, relief in her voice, Giles thought, along with sympathy.

"No, she didn't die, just, you know, went." There was a deep grief in his voice, Giles felt. He too felt a deep regret in his stomach just then. For things passed. The stirring in his groin disappeared.

"She left, I'm alone. Me and my research. I do my own thing. I live a quiet life, that's all there is to it."

"Charles, you're such an intelligent man and must have made an outstanding teacher," said Megan. "You should be proud of yourself. Hell, I'm just a secretary. You've seen the world. We all owe you a favour. My dad, he did nothing with his life. You? You're ten times the man he is."

Giles heard Charles weep. He felt sorry for the old bastard. That and just the tiniest bit jealous.

11

Benny heaved himself back down the stairs and used the torch on his mobile to guide his way down the last few steps, just to make sure. Megan welcomed the break from the relentless darkness, and she blinked into the low light as it shone in her eyes. Then she watched Benny take a heavy seat, shaking his head.

"Nothing," she said. It wasn't a question.

Benny let the light on his phone fade out again.

Megan felt the terror rising inside her, but it was a different fear. Not fear that they might all be trapped down there, starving and desperate. It was something else.

For the last five years, Megan had been the very picture of ambition. Sharp edges and power suits. Nothing would get in her way. Now she feared it was all show. That deep down, she was already on the verge of giving up. She was going crazy down here and was afraid - no, terrified - that she just wouldn't be able to cope.

Cope with this. A slow wait until death.

It was the first time she'd seriously considered the idea she might not survive this. She cried again, but it wasn't hysterical. She tried to hide from the others her gentle sob of grief.

A dim white light appeared and just for a second Megan's heart leapt and she felt blood rushing again to her head. Then it died back down just as quickly with the realisation it was just Giles' phone.

"I'm going down," said Giles, and the light from his phone danced around the chamber as he moved around and pulled himself up to standing.

Megan could see Benny shaking his head again. He said: "What are you going to go down in all that…" He trailed off.

"That piss and shit," said Megan. Her bluntness surprised her, but she knew it was simply something other than the helplessness she had just felt. She dug her nails into her palms, trying to push that feeling of fear away again. She wouldn't give up.

"It won't do any good," said Benny. "Turn the light off, Giles. I went up as far as I could. I said two hundred steps, but I went three hundred. I got to two hundred and couldn't bear to turn around, had to keep going just in case."

"Exactly, so now I'll go down and do the same," said Giles, taking his first steps. He held out the white glow in front of him.

"Don't you see?" said Benny. There was an edge of anger in his voice now. "This isn't normal. I've been to bad places. I've seen some bad shit. But this is something else. We will not get out of here by walking up and down again and again. We have to try something else. That, or wait for someone else to find us."

Megan felt a shaking rising in her chest and tried to push it down again.

The white light swung round and lit up Giles' face. He

was looking into his phone. "Look it's 1.45am. Time's still going, still ticking on. We can do something for ourselves."

Megan could hear in his tone that Giles wasn't convinced by what he was saying.

"Look, I don't know, okay?" For the first time, Benny was almost shouting. There was a manic stiffness to his voice, like he was going to lash out. "But we should stick together. So, just sit down and turn off that light."

Giles' phone faded out again, and another shuffle confirmed he'd sat back on his step. He let out a faint grumble. A moment passed before Benny spoke again.

"What I do know is that I'm dead tired. I've just got to get some sleep. I'm hungry, I'm thirsty. My head is totally full. I need to rest and I suggest you do the same."

"Don't leave me alone, Benny," the shake in Megan's voice had returned. Giles' questions before had left her uncomfortable.

"No one is going anywhere, we're all here," said Benny. His voice had returned to gentle. His breathing had become more reassuring. "Let's all just sleep. We can talk about it in the morning."

"The morning! What does that even mean?" spat Giles. "It's just a clock ticking. In this dark, there *is* no morning. There is no night, there is no day."

"Mate, you do what you like. Me, Megan and Charles are staying here. I've got to sleep."

Giles said nothing. There was a deep tiredness in his voice when he eventually replied. "There's barely any battery in my phone now, anyway."

Megan lay down from where she sat, trying to fold her body up the next few steps above her and using her small handbag as an uncomfortable pillow.

She should stay awake, she should think. How could she

sleep with all this going on? But she had to stay in control. The slightest relaxation of concentration would have the panic rising in her again.

Despite not wanting to, she gave in to the pulling from the depths of her whole body. She dreamed of interviews, and Tube trains, and old skirts, and daylight. The deepest sleep enveloped her.

12

Filthy old bugger.

That is what they had called him at school. No pupil ever said it to his face, but he knew it was one of his nicknames. They said it in the distance behind his back, just loud enough for him to pick it up. *Here comes the filthy bugger*. In class, the kids sneezed loudly, but he could always hear 'Lechy Lawrence' in their voices behind it.

A few of the more confident boys asked loaded questions in his history classes. The corner of their mouths turned up on one side.

"Columbus took advantage of the native women when he arrived in the New World, didn't he Mr Lawrence?"

"The explorers brought some of them back on the ships, didn't they, sir? Long journey for a bunch of men. Must have been a while since they had any company, eh, Mr Lawrence?"

Every couple of months, Charles came into class to find a crude picture on the blackboard. A stick man, with flyaway hair, a big nose and glasses. In one hand the stick man would be holding a badly drawn magazine with boobs on the cover, in the other he would be would be holding his penis. The class sat there silent, blank looks on their faces as they stared intensely at their work. Charles rubbed the picture from the blackboard without a word.

Things were different back then. You meant nothing by it. Maybe he brushed a little close to some girls in his class, put a hand on their backs as they filed out of the classroom. He might have been a bit too quick to lean over their shoulders to check their history timelines.

He was the caring teacher.

He *thought* about some girls around the school in that way. But only the older ones. Those who waved it in your face. Any man would. Anyway, he was happily married. It was a long time since he and Felicity had regularly got physical, but that was the same for all middle-aged couples.

"I'm too old for that," Felicity would laugh as she would affectionately pat him away and turn back to her magazine. There were occasional bumps in the night, but they never actually *talked* about sex. It was functional. Invisible.

Rachel was the one girl who did have something special about her. She was quiet, intelligent. She had a sparkle in her eyes. She wasn't like some of the other girls. The ones with push-up bras and makeup. The ones he would think about in bed when Felicity had turned on her side and fallen asleep.

Rachel was appealing exactly because she wasn't like those other girls. She was there to learn, and genuinely looked up to Charles. She seemed to be as interested in his subject as he was. She called him Sir.

She *liked* him.

He thought she liked him. It had all been a mistake, of course. She'd asked for help with coursework at lunchtime and the class had cleared quickly. Everyone was off to watch a fight between two bruisers on the main field. The planned scrap had been the talk of the secondary school all morning.

But Rachel was more interested in her school work. He welcomed the chance to help her. But he'd leaned in a bit too close. Put his hands where they shouldn't have been.

"No," she said, and went to get out of her chair. She pushed him off with those soft pink hands - no nasty nail varnish, Charles thought - but the twinkle was still in her eyes. She had such a sweet little voice, innocent. Not common like the other girls. The way they shouted between chomps of chewing gum.

He pushed her back down into her seat. Pushed his hands against her breast, buried his nose into the top of her head. Drew in the floral scent of her shampoo.

"No," she said. "No, Sir." And that was it.

Rachel was gone. She'd left the door swinging as she'd disappeared into the corridor.

The next day she didn't come into school. That afternoon, the school secretary delivered the note: could Mr Lawrence please pop in to see the head teacher during last period.

No one mentioned Rachel, or even that Charles had done anything wrong. But it was made clear. Letchy Lawrence's gardening leave would start tomorrow. He left angry that his career had been cut short. That he'd been thrown onto the scrap heap when he still had so much to share with his pupils.

He knew he couldn't fight it. He had to let it go, and become satisfied with spending more time with Felicity. Hang around until his pension came through. He'd had a good innings.

Charles shifted his body on the steps and felt himself

drifting back off to sleep. He'd been weeping since the lights went out, but really he'd done all his crying long ago.

'*Sorry Felicity. Sorry Rachel.*'

He'd never said it out loud to anyone, and now there was no longer anyone to say it to. His heart ached.

Letchy Lawrence. And now it was all loneliness. The absence of everything. Not just here on the staircase, but outside, too. He heard snoring from above. He opened his eyes and peered into the blackness. Then he closed them again.

Was there light up there somewhere? Somehow, he didn't care one way or the other.

13

Bernard Harris sat in the back of the police van with a bloody graze across his face and pain in both his arms. They had been twisted behind his back and they were still fixed together with cuffs. The graze was from where his face hit the ground after an officer had yanked him out of the car and slammed him into the pavement.

The police had been armed, fully padded up like futuristic soldiers. From the moment he saw them, Bernard knew it was over. Their Renault had hardly come to a stop before he and Punky had thrown their guns out of the window and held up their hands in surrender, just like the Asian chap in the petrol station had minutes before. The two cop cars had all but run them off the road, one to the right and one close behind, inching them closer to the pavement, threatening to collide.

After that, everything had happened quickly. Bernard had opened the door himself, his hands in the air, but a white cop had torn him to the floor, slammed a boot between his shoulders and pointed a gun into the back of his neck. Another came over with one more heavy boot to drop onto his lower back, just for good measure. There was a lot of shouting, a lot of swearing, a lot of hard grit on the floor.

After four or five minutes of eating dirt, a third officer had come over to yank Bernard's arms behind his back and lock them in place. Then they lifted him off the floor, grabbing under his shoulders, twisting his arms even further and pushed his head down painfully towards the floor. He was thrown into the back of the police van, which had just screeched up behind where the three cars had clustered.

Bernard welcomed it. The cravings had gone, momentarily replaced by adrenaline. The excitement of the 'getaway' and the ruckus of being taken down by the police. He knew the cravings would come back, but for now he was happy to just sit on the hard bench. He relished the moment of peace, even though his head was pounding, his face hurt and his heart was pumping blood furiously into every inch of his body.

He just wanted to rest.

He woke up the next morning on a hard blue mattress in a cell at Ilford Police Station. He'd given his name and details the night before to the custody sergeant. Then he had been cautioned and told a duty solicitor would arrive tomorrow morning.

The police could hold him for up to 48 hours before any charges, the sergeant had said, but let's be honest: with the CCTV, the police car footage and the testimony of four police officers plus the Sri Lankan station attendant, it's unlikely to take that long.

Bernard peered around the grey-tiled cell, trying to take in every inch of his surroundings, hoping to put off the inevitable: the deep need, the craving, the sickening desperation for a hit. An hour later he was banging on the metal door, crying through the grate, until an officer came to tell him to calm down.

Two hours later, Bernard had told the police he was a heroin addict and desperately needed something. When the duty solicitor arrived, he took one look at Bernard and asked for him to be given medical help.

Pleading not-guilty was never an option. He'd gone to the Magistrates' court to confirm his details, but armed robbery was too serious to be dealt with at Magistrates' level. He'd been sent temporarily to prison until his Crown Court case came up.

Plead guilty and you'll get three years, probably out in eighteen months. You'll be put through a drug rehabilitation programme, the solicitor had urged him. Bernard didn't want to go to prison for 18 months and he definitely didn't want to come off the drugs. But it didn't seem like anyone was going to give him a choice about either. So he pleaded guilty.

The Crown Court judge gave him six years.

14

In the dark, half asleep, Giles thought about something he hadn't laid out on the steps when Megan had demanded it this morning. It was an empty blister, which had carried two small tablets.

Giles had remembered to take the first one, just before Megan had called for the show-and-tell and popped it with a little Lucozade on one of his trips to the toilet. Then, with more difficulty, he'd taken the other late afternoon, with no liquid at all. It has stuck in his throat and Giles had had to wait until the little mucus in his throat had dissolved the starch outer, so he could swallow the revolting tasting tablet.

He'd been on the pills, or at least one version of them, since not long after university.

There's an old saying at Cambridge. Whatever you do there, you do it to extremes. If you're into your studies, then you work very hard and come out with a first and probably stay on for a post-grad. If you're into playing the flute, or the violin, or the piano, you spend every spare moment practicing and play with the university orchestra. If you're into student politics, then you spend your life on the streets or in fraught meetings with political opponents or chaining your-self to the Vice Chancellor's front gate.

For Giles it was the good times. Drinking, a bit of drugs, late nights, incredible highs followed by disastrous hang-overs and an empty feeling of self-loathing.

For three years, it seemed, Giles was either out in pubs or nightclubs, or lying in bed in dark rooms, staring at the wall, not wanting to get up, not wanting to see anyone, not wanting to work or even eat.

Essays were handed in late or not at all. Giles rarely attended lectures and was boisterous and bullying in student seminars, or withdrawn and cold, not even answering when his tutors asked him direct questions. Just university life, thought Giles.

A problem, thought his tutors. Twice they'd tried to rusticate him: to throw him out of the university. But each time, Giles had come through. He handed in his essay at the last minute or managed to sweet-talk the rustication committee, recovering a just-in-time natural charm. He'd scraped through with a Desmond: a 2-2 degree that meant, academically at least, he might as well not have gone at all. But still, he had Cambridge on his CV. And that meant a lot in the City.

It wasn't just university life. Out of college, he'd moved with a few of his university mates into a crappy terrace in Hackney, rented from a dodgy landlord who demanded 12 signed cheques up front. The drinking and drugs continued. But while his mates trooped off the next day to their milk-round jobs in London, relatively recovered from the previous night's excesses, his hangovers were always the worst.

He'd say he couldn't face work. He knew he couldn't face anything.

A few times in that first year after uni, the friends he lived with came back to find Giles wasn't there. For days he'd be gone, no phone calls, no texts. He'd return with a huge grin, a crate of beer and money for pizzas all round. He'd been at his parent's house, or staying with his brother, or saying he'd scored with a girl and had been too busy to call in. Then it was all backslapping and back to the pub.

One Christmas it was particularly lively. The Hackney House, as they called it, threw a massive seasonal bash. All the Cambridge-to-London expats from their year were invited, the alcohol and the drugs were in abundance. The music was so loud and went on so late that even the neighbours had been pushed over their Christmas tolerance, been round a few times and then called the police. Officers made a good natured visit around 3 a.m., knocked on the door and told Giles and his stumbling mates it was probably about time to round things up.

They sat in their marked Sierra outside the terrace, and half-an-hour later the lights inside dimmed and the music stopped. A few left for taxis, the night bus or houses nearby. A handful sat around the living room smoking the last of the spliffs and drinking whisky, determined to stay up until morning. Most floated off around the house, finding sofas and floors and anywhere else where beds weren't already packed four or more-across with passed-out bodies.

The next morning a light revelry continued, albeit more sedate. Someone was frying up bacon. A few were gamely cracking cans of Carlsberg, but drinking them without genuine conviction. One by one, the remaining partygoers rose to join the party debrief, and no one was surprised that Giles was still missing by noon when the consensus emerged that lunch would be taken at the Princess of Wales down by the canal.

A few pints of IPA would send the group on their various ways around the country to spend Christmas with their family. When the time came, someone popped upstairs to wake Giles and tell him the plan. They found him in just boxer shorts on top of the covers, shaking and kicking out at the walls. When they tried to calm him, he lashed out at them too, screeching and crying, biting into bloody lips, his toes covered in blood from the kicking.

The ambulance took ages to come: there had been any number of Christmas party detritus for the paramedics to clear up that morning. Giles was just the latest, but once they'd seen Giles' state, they'd called the police for backup. With the officers, the paramedics strapped Giles to the gurney, and an officer had travelled in the back to watch over him. At A&E the doctors had immediately sedated him, sending Giles into a deep sleep while the night before dissipated from his system.

When he came round on the ward, a few friends were at his bedside. They joshed him uncomfortably about pushing it too far. It would be a party to go down in history: one that had been so kicking that Giles had actually ended up in hospital.

But Giles just lay on his side, stared out of the window at the grey afternoon sky until they'd given up. They said they'd call his folks, then headed off to their families. Giles didn't say goodbye. Or Merry Christmas.

Giles had been the wildest of the bunch last night, jumping around to the music and challenging everyone in sight with tequila shots, kissing and trying to grope the girls. A severe case of alcohol poisoning, they concluded.

The consultant who found a moment in her schedule to see Giles in his hospital bed that evening concluded differently. The duty psychologist who came to see him next morning would end up being the same one who Giles would see every six months for the next five years as they tweaked his meds, trying to smooth out the creases of his mood swings.

They talked about how he had always been in trouble at boarding school: the biting and lashing out during rugby matches. They talked about how he had liked to be the centre of attention, playing up for the teachers and for the girls. They talked about university and his friends, about panicking over essays and deadlines that got him so worked up he'd bang the wall with his fists.

He'd burned himself with a cigarette. The voices in his head had told him to.

They talked about the early years after university, when some days he'd sit at his desk at his sales job with his head in his hands, wishing for the day to be over, but on others could leap around a client's boardroom getting them so excited about some crappy piece of software that really could change the way the company worked, forever!

Giles was released from hospital, and his father came to pick him up. A panic attack brought on by too much booze, he'd told his folks with a thin smile.

He was planning a quiet Christmas this year, he said, and spent most of the time in his room. On New Year he cried off the festivities with his old school friends. He had a stomach bug. His folks never let on what the doctor had told them in a private room, just before they'd seen him.

Bi-polar disorder is a particular mental illness, one more frequent in younger adults than those younger adults care to admit. It's depression, but it's marked by incredible highs and excess: overt happiness, particular sociability, generosity, behaviour that seems to lack tact and social awareness. But those periods of elation are followed by devastating lows: the black dogs as black as they can get. Voices. Self-loathing. Physical pain, invented by the brain.

The drugs helped, at least when his medical team found the right ones and the right dose. But Giles had to remember to take them. Morning and afternoon.

"A missed pill here and there won't matter too much, but just keep taking them," Doctor Potts had told him. "Don't come off the drugs completely, and definitely not too quickly. And try to ease off the booze, and any recreational drugs."

It wasn't that they would clash with the anti-depressants. It was that Giles was more likely to neglect to take them too many times, lifting him into a high that made him think he no longer needed them, or a low so deep he didn't care if he took them or not.

Over the last five years, Giles had fallen off the wagon only three times. A year before he'd met Lisa, his room-mate at boarding school had died. It was Hodgkins Disease, a cancer caught too late. The two had kept in touch, but hadn't been that close. But it was the first time someone Giles knew well had died. Simon had been Giles's age, maybe just a few months older. It was impossible that he wasn't around anymore. That all those times, all that growing up together, had been for nothing.

Absolutely nothing.

And if that could happen to anyone, well, what was the point? It took a brief stay in an acute mental health ward and two months of bi-weekly meetings with Doctor Potts to get Giles back on the anti-depressants and back on an even keel.

To Giles' knowledge, there were only three people in the world apart from his parents who knew Giles was bi-polar - though he still refused to use the term - and one was Giles himself. It's not something you mention at work. Not if you wanted to succeed. Another was Doctor Potts (and Giles supposed some other doctors working with her, but they didn't count.) The other was Lisa. She didn't find out until three months after she'd moved in with him.

Giles hid the meds from her and, because they weren't there in the bathroom every morning and evening, it was too easy to forget to take them.

Once, about six months after she'd moved in, Giles had fallen out of the habit of taking his meds. He'd found himself more frequently going on drinking binges with old university buddies. That turned into drinking with anyone who'd go out with him. Sometimes, he drank alone.

Then he'd come home at 2 a.m. and play music at top volume, overturning the furniture and tossing crockery around the room as if it was some manic game.

Then for two weeks he'd lain on the sofa and refused to go to work. All the guys were doing better than he was, they were all on the up. He was shit. What did he have?

What he had was Lisa.

She knew Giles well enough to see something wasn't right with this picture. Sure, she too went out with her friends, but this was something else. This wasn't the charming, relaxed boy who'd leant back in his chair and invited her for tassels and tagine at a Moroccan restaurant. At the end of Giles' second week of calling in sick, she'd taken the day off herself and spent the day with him on the sofa, holding Giles' head in her lap. He'd lain there silently. Then he'd wept. Then he'd cried.

"I'm not who you think I am," said Giles. "I'm nothing, just a failure. You deserve more. I won't blame you if you go."

"I'm not going anywhere," Lisa said. "You've got me." It

seemed to make him cry harder. She said it over and over: "You've got me, you've got me, you've got me."

She held him in her arms, rocking him, crying too.

"I'll always be here for you, no matter what," she promised.

And so Giles told her. He told her about the party, about the psychologist, about Simon, about the meds. He showed her the prescription, the blister of little pills. They looked up his drugs on the internet, followed the links to bi-polar disorder and read the symptoms together.

On Monday morning, he went back to work. On Tuesday, he gave her the number for Doctor Potts. On Wednesday, Lisa put his drugs on the shelf above the bathroom sink, next to their toothbrushes.

That's where they stayed until Lisa left.

You've got me, you've got me, you've got me.

Liar, liar, liar.

15

It was Megan that noticed it first. She could have been asleep for hours, but it felt like days. The first feelings were the painful stiffness in her neck, and her ear ringing where it had pressed against her handbag for hours.

Then as she swallowed, she felt the gritty soreness of her dry throat. But as she rose her head and blinked her eyes, there was a feeling of something different. Something had changed. She shook her head and looked around her.

The lights had come back on.

The others blinked into the light moments after Megan, and there was groaning and yawning as they shook themselves awake. Giles looked down for a moment into Megan's eyes, which were red and a little crusted. Her cheek had a deep crease in it, where the handle of her bag had been. He looked for a moment more, then spun round to look up at Benny.

Benny had sat up and was staring at the ceiling, nodding

slightly, the shadow of a puzzled smile on his flaking lips. No one needed to speak, and they sat there for a moment taking deep breaths as if they were gasping in fresh air.

"Wake up Charlie Boy, we've got news."

Giles called down past Megan where Charles was still sleeping. He winced as his dry voice came out high and croaky, just like it had been in his early teens. He looked around the chamber, a grin growing on his face.

He lit a cigarette, blew smoke around with satisfaction. Six more in the box.

"Well, I don't know about you, but I'm going to get a coffee. Who wants a croissant?"

He noticed a little laugh from Megan, as she rubbed her palms up and down her face to bring herself into wakefulness. He looked at his watch. It was 5.15 a.m. His first thought was that it felt like he'd slept for more than the four hours he had. His second was that it was still very early morning.

Morning.

"Hold on," he said, turning to Benny. "Morning. This matters. It's Tube time."

Benny looked back, his face unmoved.

"The first Tubes go through at this time. They've switched the lights on. There's someone there. We *must* be part of the network, just lost somewhere in the depths."

Giles pulled himself up by the bannister and stretched his legs. He looked around at Megan and Benny, whose faces now showed they were working it out for themselves.

The lights had gone out after midnight last night, now they'd come on again at five. The times the London Underground shuts up its stations, then opens them up again next day.

Light means people. There must be someone sitting in a control box somewhere, flicking switches, bringing the underground to life. Giles looked around for a camera. Staircases and escalators had cameras, didn't they? But they'd all checked for them, for anything, for hours yesterday. Still.

"It's going to be okay," he whispered, almost to himself. Then louder, "Jesus, I thought we were dead, but it's going to be okay."

Megan pulled herself up too and rearranged her skirt at the waist. She wiggled her toes, one by one, as if she was working pins and needles out of her feet and legs.

"I've got to *go,*" she said.

"Ha, no need for that," said Giles. "We'll just walk up. Like I say, we're part of the network. There *has* to be a top to this."

"No Giles, I've really *got* to go. I didn't, well, you know, I didn't. Yesterday. I couldn't." She dipped her head low and looked away.

Not my cup of tea, Giles, but hey: whatever you're into, mate, whatever you're into.

It wasn't what Giles was into. He forced the thought away, and gently banged his hand against the wall, enjoying the distraction the pain offered.

"I need to get out of here," Giles said, breaking the discomfort. "I'm going up, further than any of us have been before. The lights show that the world is out there. There must be something: an emergency exit, a camera."

Time to lose these losers.

Benny shook his head. He'd been up and up and up.

"The lights had come back on, but none of this changes things," he said.

"Well, I've decided I'm going to keep on up until I find something." Giles blew out smoke, turned, and headed upward.

"Do you think Giles is right?" said Megan eventually. "Could he find something up there and just not come back?"

"No, I don't," said Benny. "He might be right about us being trapped and the outside world going on without us, but I don't think he's going to find the top of this spiral. Things just aren't looking that way.

"Going up and down these steps isn't going to change our situation."

"Like a ship lost far out at sea," said Megan. "No one knows you're missing, don't even know where to look for you, until they pick up your S.O.S. signal. Like yesterday, banging on the rail. Then suddenly everything slots together."

"Yeah, and then you're rescued," he turned around and looked down the corridor before him. He looked up at the lights lining the top of the corridor, grubby black circles of glass sunk into the tiles. He stood and reached up, easily tall enough to touch the lights. He fingered the cold discs, running his finger around the circles. His fingers were grimy when he withdrew them.

"The lights went off last night and back on this morning," Benny said. "They could be on a timer, or someone is switching them off. Either way, if lights go out when they're not supposed to, it must make a signal somewhere. A flashing red light."

"So, you want to smash the light and plunge us into darkness on the off chance?"

"No," said Benny. "But I could take the light out, look at the wires. Maybe break the connection, at least for a moment. Or for a couple of moments, one after the other: S.O.S. again."

"God, it's worth a shot," Megan said. Benny noticed in her a hint of excitement.

"S.O.S.," said Charles from below, now awake. "The old ones are the good ones."

A voice came from above, as Giles rounded the corner: "And exactly how do you propose to do that?"

"With this," the builder replied. He was holding up a large screwdriver.

16

G iles shouted: "What the fuck, Benny? Why didn't you tell us you had a screwdriver? We could have been digging ourselves out of here."

"Digging out?" said Benny, his voice sharp.

"Yeah, yesterday. When we were all running round like maniacs, banging on walls, trying to scratch off the tiles with our fingernails. We could have been smashing through them with that.

"What else do you have in that little tool bag? An axe? A fucking crowbar? We've been here for 24 hours hours, and only now do you reveal you have brought a Black and Decker workbench to the party?"

"Don't you think I've thought about that," said Benny, stern again. "All I have is this screwdriver. Don't you think I've spent every moment down in this pit thinking about getting out of here?

"But dig where, Giles? Dig with a screwdriver? This isn't The Shawshank Redemption. This is real life." Benny stopped, as if reconsidering what he'd just said.

Benny continued, more wearily now: "There will be

three feet or more of concrete behind the tiles, and then beyond that just solid earth. There's no getting out that way, and definitely not with a screwdriver."

"How do you know that? It could be just a foot?" said Giles.

"Man, I know about walls. Thick ones. There's no digging out." He held up the tool. It was a hand's breadth long, slightly thicker than a pencil and tapered into a flat head at the end. Giles had to admit it was hardly a pneumatic drill.

"Well, cards on the table, Benny, what else have you in your builder's bag of tricks?"

Benny pulled open his little leather bag and showed it to Giles, then to Megan and Charles. There was nothing. A few screws, some long plastic cable ties, a blunt pencil. Not much of a builder.

"I'm not allowed to take tools home," he said. His voice was uncomfortable. "I took the screwdriver and some screws from the site this morning to fix a railing at home. Nothing much gets done where I live. I was going to return it."

Benny sounded like a school kid, the tone of apology in his voice as if he'd stepped out of line.

Poor Benny. Please don't give me detention, Miss. I'll be a really good boy.

If he was honest with himself, Giles was jealous that he hadn't thought to exploit the lights. He was supposed to have the brains, Benny the brawn.

Nice one, Brain of Britain. Yeah, real clever.

His workmates had said it to him, jokingly - it was always a joke, wasn't it? - after a team meeting last week. He'd suggested a new way of time-managing that had fallen flat with Andy Asswipe.

At least he'd tried, instead of hanging round doing the

same old thing, taking every opportunity to bunk off or to look busy while doing nothing.

"So, how's this going to work, Benny," said Megan. "I don't see any screws in the lights."

"No, the light will be cemented in behind the tiles. Tamper proof. That way they last longer. That's why there are no wires either. Someone could pull them down. The wires will be behind the tiles too."

He stood and reached up to poke around the light above him with the screwdriver, seeing if there was any crack he could jam into, to get some purchase.

"Are you sure you know what you're doing," asked Giles. "Because if those lights go out for good we're totally stuffed."

Benny sat down again, obviously reconsidering. Giles and Megan looked at each other.

"I don't think it'll work like that," said Benny. He didn't sound convinced. "They should be on a parallel circuit. Who knows how many lights are on the line, but you wouldn't normally have all of them in the whole staircase connected. Just a dozen or so at a time. If one goes out, we take out that many lights. But not the whole staircase. So, the worst case would be that we just move 100 steps up the staircase and use the light there."

"Yeah, what he just said," said Giles, admitting defeat.

"You're a clever man, Benny," said Charles. "It's good to have you on board."

"You learn these things, where I've been. In the trade. And elsewhere."

Benny stood again and held the screwdriver up to the tiles surrounding the light. He used the palm of his hand to bang the point of it into the grouting between them, but nothing came away. He tried different angles and started to hammer in heavy blows with his palm. But still the screwdriver made just tiny dents in the grouting, or just slipped off the tiles with a painful-to-hear screech.

Benny sat down again, his arms hurting from holding them above his head. But he untied a shoelace on the hefty boot on his right foot. He pulled it off and stood up again.

This time he had more power behind the screwdriver as he brought the heel of the boot hard into the handle. A few screeches more, a few more dents, and then a shard of grey tile flew away and hit the wall. Benny brought the tip of the tool to where the shard had come loose, and hammered again, this time causing a crack about an inch long.

Benny took a breath, then raised the boot and the screwdriver again. More and more chips and shards were coming away from the tile, allowing Benny to get underneath them. With one heavy boot blow, a whole tile came away revealing - in just one corner - the rusty edge of a small circle of metal.

"We're in," he said.

Benny sat down.

"Should I have a go?" Giles asked, limply. He knew he wasn't tall enough. Benny was struggling to keep his own muscly arms above his head.

It went unsaid.

Benny continued, taking rests every couple of minutes. He had been right: behind the tiles was just grey concrete and that was staying fast as each boot blow tore away chunks of tile. But as the tiles fell away around the light fitting, more of the rusted metal collar came into view.

By the time enough collar had been revealed for him to prise the screwdriver underneath it, he was sweating, breathing heavily and his attacks at the tile had become shorter. The metal moved and bent slightly where Benny had stuck the tool underneath it. With a bit more force, it would come away. He gave the metal another lever, a final bit of tile moved and the light casing popped out.

Benny pulled his hands down, dropped the boot and massaged his biceps, flexing his hands, which had become stiff from the work.

The three of them looked up to the ceiling. The light hung there. It was a cone of metal, with the glass disc at one end still lit. The cone tapered into two flat edges, where it met two thick black wires, which ran back into the hole the light had fallen from.

"So, now we just break the glass and unscrew the light-bulb," said Giles.

"I don't know," said Benny, looking up again and handling the light. "I don't think it'll be as simple as that. They look like LEDs. They'll be soldered in. I'll need to disconnect then re-connect the wires."

For the first time, Benny thought this was madness. But he knew too that if he didn't do something, Giles would probably have a go and might end up killing himself.

His plan was to tear away the rubber on one cable. There, it would connect with the light bulb by either being soldered to it, or running through a hole and tied off.

If Benny could get one wire disconnected from the bulb, the light would go off. And hopefully a dozen or more lights, signifying to the outside world they were down there. Touch it back onto the plates, and the light would come back on again.

S.O.S.

But if he touched both the metal light casing and the uncovered wire at the same time with bare hands, his arms might become the conductor of who knows how many volts of electricity. And he didn't fancy finding out.

"I need something to hold the light with, to stop my fingers touching the metal."

"Why?" asked Megan.

Benny decided not to tell the truth: that one wrong move might not only electrocute him, but would also plunge them all into darkness for many metres all around, with next to no chance of reconnecting the light in pitch black without getting electrocuted. That's if he could even find the light.

"The bulb will get hot when I'm working with it," he said.

Giles held up his tie.

"Something thicker," he said. "How about your jacket?"

"This is Shepherd and Woodward, it would be a crime," said Giles.

"Just pass me the damn jacket," Benny said.

Giles took it off and passed it up. Benny stuck the screwdriver into one sleeve and tore a hole. Then with some tugging, he ripped the whole sleeve right away.

He flung the jacket at Giles.

"Here, you can sell it at a 25 percent discount."

Giles rolled it into a ball, apparently embarrassed to put the jacket back on.

Benny passed his mobile to Megan, and showed her how to turn on the screen torch. When the lights go out, she'd need to shine it where Benny was working so he could connect the wires back again to create the S.O.S.

He put his arm through Giles' sleeve, making a kind of glove with his fingers. He reached up for the light.

17

M egan Lisk looked in the mirror and considered her outfit.

She'd been trying on different skirts from seven a.m, and if she didn't do something radical and actually decide pretty soon, she was going to be late for her interview.

She eventually went back to the first skirt she'd pulled on that morning, over skin colour tights. The skirt was tight, but at least it wasn't faded and bobbly like the ones she'd been wearing to her job - her old job, she hoped - for the last month or so.

She couldn't be late for today's interview. Not a minute. In fact, she needed to be 10 minutes early, looking pristine and ready to take on the world.

Megan wasn't naturally confident. At school in Epping, she had spent much of her life in other people's shadows: at school, she was a quiet girl who diligently got on with her work, trying to ignore the boys who seemed to become more rowdy and crude as their voices became more grimy, their hair more greasy and their face speckled with grubby patches of fluff and puddles of red spots.

But as hard as she tried, and as much as she tried to act like them, she couldn't match the grades some of the other girls achieved. Or receive the attention - was it affection? - the teachers lathered them with.

Her dad urged her not to push herself too far. He said she should do things normal for her age, not always be studying or reading in her room.

Find a boyfriend (but not a drop out), go for a day out (but only to where I tell you), be a rebel (but do what I tell you). What was education for anyway, when there were so many local jobs around?

Dad didn't have to have any 'aspiration', as the school posters were always telling Megan she needed. He had been a general builder, just like his own father. He'd grown up on the tools. Had no training, an interview, or had even got close to a CV in his life. Anything else, well, that wasn't even on his radar.

Dad knew nothing about the jobs market. Particularly for young women. He pictured women behind shopping tills, in beauty parlours, serving at Iceland or the ice cream shops. It never occurred to him Megan might wish for something more.

And if he even considered it, well, she knew where that was going: he'd hate it. Megan would leave Epping. College. University. Maybe a job in London. She wouldn't be there for dinner each night. She wouldn't sit on the sofa with him, watching the TV programmes he wanted to watch. She wouldn't have to tell him her every move, get approval for every time she went out, with a clock ticking for her return.

She had only got her own house key when she was 15.

So, of course, Megan did exactly what her dad didn't want. She *was* rebelling. She was determined to work hard and get out of there. The suffocating home. The oppressive lack of expectation.

So Megan worked. She worked really hard. Months before her GCSEs she buried her head in her books, skipping TV so she could keep pushing.

"You can study too hard, you know," Dad said. "Then it'll stop going in. There's only so much your head can cram."

What did he know? His parents had always had an improbable amount of money. Dad drove around in his little white van fixing people's toilets, tut-tutting at their boilers.

How could you fill up your day with that, when there never seemed to be enough time for Megan to get all the study in that she wanted? Yet Dad lived in a comfortable semi-detached in a quiet leafy street. No debts, no mortgage.

No desire to see what lay outside his little suburb, let alone the world.

"I'm comfortable," Dad would say. "I just look after my girl and my precious collection of chilli plants. What else does a Dad need? You don't need to do anything. Waste of your time. Waste of my money."

It was a different message from what Megan was hearing at school. The teachers were always on about succeeding, the challenge of getting a job, bright new futures for those who got their heads down.

Only so much of that stuck. What was more worrying was the occasional conversations among her friends: about brothers and sisters who were at university, racking up debt, not knowing how they were going to get rid of it, nor what they were going to do afterwards with no money to start their life with.

Dad didn't know the half of it. Megan was glad.

And so she continued to study. But it wasn't enough. Not without someone pushing her, like the other kids' folks did.

Megan missed out on the GCSE grades she needed to continue onto A-levels. The teachers had assured her it would be fine, but Megan didn't feel they backed it up with the encouragement they offered the more 'promising' girls. Dad was right. Better get her details dropped into Superdrug.

Instead, Megan left school and the sixth form behind. The just-missed GCSEs fired her up. She wanted to prove her teachers wrong. Her Dad too.

Mostly, herself.

She headed for the local vocational college. It was far from what she'd hoped: all courses in hairdressing and nail work, car mechanics for the boys. A bunch of NVQs in secretarial skills.

This course aims to teach basic skills, offering opportunities to gain employment in administration and secretarial work in settings such as solicitors, finance, new technologies. With emphasis on good presentation, attention to detail, basic word processing skills and customer relations.

That was it.

That was an entire year's course description, printed alongside a stock image picture of a 20-something girl in a smart suit, in thick ringed black glasses with a pen poised over a notebook.

No woman around the college looked like that.

Here it was all tracksuits and scraped back hair. Or else inch-thick makeup, fake tans and animal prints. Megan downloaded the course syllabus, but it was more of the same.

Lots of words and promises, but between the lines, it was a lack of expectation: just turn up to the courses, get the CV points, then work in a travel agency.

It was that or do the rounds of Epping and surrounds,

asking around in bakers and bathroom shops, tanning salons and pubs - oh please, not pubs - to see if there were any casual shifts going.

Like with her GCSEs, Megan gritted her teeth and kept turning up every day. The class started 30 strong. By the second month, there were ten left. The course tutors were disinterested, putting in the hours with tired presentations and a monotonous tone in their voice to match.

There was no homework set, simply sheets every few weeks to take home and indicate - by circling emojis - how you thought the course was going.

At the end of each term there was a simple test, but the marks came back a mishmash. As if the tutors had picked grades at random in the five minutes before class started.

"Why don't you take it easy," her dad had said. "Cruise through. I'll offer you a job. Work the phones. I could show you how to do the invoicing. Then some rich guy will whisk you away and you'll be made."

With every word that came out of her dad's mouth, Megan was determined to work harder. To take the paltry effort the college put in and multiply it ten times.

While her classmates failed to come in, or sauntered into tutorials 15 minutes late smelling of smoke, Megan was always there early. She took detailed notes, bought extra books, spent time in the cruddy library at lunch times, instead of lounging on the grass outside or shopping for clothes on the High Street.

Every now and again an uncomfortable thought would spring up as she walked to the college.

What was she doing this for? NVQs were pass and fail (or was it 'competent' or 'not competent'?). And word was that it was impossible to fail this course.

Her CV bullet point would look exactly the same size

and shape as everyone else's at the end of the year. In those low times she had to remind herself - even said it out loud to herself sometimes - that it wasn't about the college, or the CV point. It was about getting the knowledge and skills. The NVQ was a base, something to spring off to do the real learning she needed between times.

Because while the others would use their crappy qualification to get those local jobs, she was determined to head west and into the City. To start at the bottom, demonstrate her knowledge and skills, then work upwards.

She'd seen the jobs on the employment websites: legal secretaries, financial secretaries, personal assistants. In the City you could pull in £25k, £30k a year. There were case studies of women who had started off on the front office desk and were now running teams. That's where Megan was going. At the very least.

That was where Rachel was going, too. Or at least, that's what Megan assumed.

18

Benny grasped the casing tightly through the suit material and used the screwdriver to scrape away the rubber sheath on one wire.

He was pleased to see the copper wire beneath was tied around a hole in the metal, rather than soldered onto it. It would give him more wire to work with, and a chance to tie the wire - somehow, God knows how - back onto the casing.

Tentatively Benny offered the bare wire the tiniest touch with the screwdriver. No spark. He released a short, grateful sigh. He used the tip of the screwdriver to unfold the wire until it was just sitting in the hole it was wound around. With every move, his arms ached more from holding them above his head.

Benny pocketed the screwdriver and grasped the black rubber casing of the wire. The copper wire slipped out of the hole and the whole staircase went pitch black. The same deepest dark as the night before.

"Shit," said Benny.

"What, what?" It was Megan, shouting into the blackness. In panic.

"It's okay. I just hoped the lights were on a shorter circuit. That a few lights would stay on. Megan, the phone."

The chamber was suddenly bathed in green light, and Megan held the torch up to the roof. She tried to manoeuvre it so most of the light fell where Benny was working. But everywhere there seemed to be arms and heads casting shadows.

There was just enough glow for Benny to see where to touch the bare wire back onto the bulb. He held his breath and brought the two together. The bulb came on, along with the lights running in either direction along the roof.

"Brilliant," said Giles with genuine encouragement. "Now, dot dot dot, dash dash dash."

"Give me a chance."

He pulled the wire away again, then touched it back. The lights flashed off, then on again. Then he did it again. Benny's arms were really hurting now. It felt like the blood had completely drained from them, and it was all he could do to stop them from shaking.

On-off, on-off. Touch-remove. Touch-remove. He tried to follow the S.O.S. pattern, but it was difficult to judge how long to let the dashes go on for, how short to leave a dot.

And then Benny could do no more. His arms were aching so much he felt that soon he'd have to drop them. But that would mean losing everything. He'd have to scramble around in the dark to find live wires that could electrocute him.

Somehow, he had to get the wire tied back onto the fork, and he'd have to move fast because his arms were going into spasms.

"Megan, I need more light." She moved again, trying another angle to get the glow up. Suddenly it started to fade.

"Megan, touch the screen." Benny's arms were in pain. What was left of the light swung around to her face.

"I'm trying to," she was jamming her fingers onto the screen, but a final dim green hue faded from her face and they were again plunged into darkness. The phone let out a double-beep, the unbearable sound of it switching off.

"Oh, shit," said Giles.

"Benny?" cried Megan.

"Wait, wait." He was puffing. Every moment his arms felt they would drop. There was no longer a choice. Benny released the wire and bulb and let his arms fall to his sides.

"What's going on," said Giles, his voice echoing down the chamber.

"Give me a second."

He blew out a deep breath. Massaged his arms, and flexed both of his hands. He reached into his pocket and pushed his arms back up, grasping around blindly for the light again. If he touched the bald wire itself, he still didn't know if Giles' jacket sleeve would protect him. Or whether the electricity would blast his shoulder out of its socket.

The chamber went completely silent. Benny's breathing stopped all together.

Then there was a spark. He let out a high cry and fell back.

The lights came on just in time for the others to see Benny's leg slip, his ankle twist awkwardly off a step and for him to fall backwards down the stairs. Benny's back hit the ground hard. His twisted body rumbled down the spiral for two or three steps, grazing his back, before the smacking of his head against the wall eventually broke his trajectory. Benny felt a thick thud across his whole body as his head met tile and an enormous whack echoed around the chamber.

Benny threw his arms up over his head, clinging tightly to the spot that had hit the wall, letting out a huge cry as he swung around into a sitting position. He rocked his head up and down, swearing under his breath. A deep pain throbbed at the back of his head and pulsated around his skull and into his face. His vision was blurred, and he saw shoots of light behind his eyes.

"Ahh, fuck, fuck," cried Benny, which seemed to help. He felt the tension ease from his body.

Megan sprang up first, with Giles following behind. She plonked herself next to Benny and put her arms around him, pulling his entire head and arms tightly into her chest.

"Shit, shit, shit."

"Benny, are you okay?" she said.

He didn't answer. His brain felt like a dead weight rattling round in a box, and for a moment Benny's thoughts sprang this way and that; memories and songs; pictures and words. Walls, a woman, a petrol station, Stevie, the spiral staircase, the smell of cigarettes, a cold shower, a building site. All jumbled up, trying to slot themselves back into his mind in proper order.

His rattling brain bashing around like a bell in a child's toy. It eventually came to rest.

"I said are you okay, Benny?" said Megan.

"Yeah, I think so," he said. "Bloody hell, that hurt." He felt the tension easing.

"Shit, you okay, mate?" said Giles, who'd followed Megan down to where Benny had fallen. He'd just missed Charles, who was now sitting just a few steps up from the others.

"Just let me look," Megan said, releasing Benny and

pushing her fingers up to where his own were grasping the back of his head. He resisted at first, then slowly released his grip to allow her.

"There's no blood," she said.

"At least that's something," said Benny, who now felt the deep throbbing being replaced by an excruciating ache surrounding his head. He grunted at the stabbing pain as Megan touched around the area at the back.

"There are no cracks or dents," she said. She could feel skin pulled taught over his head that was already becoming mushy to her touch, rising into a bruise. "It's okay, I think."

"Well, it doesn't feel okay, I can tell you that much," but Benny let out a little laugh to reassure her.

"Anywhere else hurt?" asked Giles, "You went down pretty hard."

"No, I don't think so. Battered and bruised." Benny shook different parts of his body, searching for pain. He'd done the same a few times, after taking a beating during recess when he was a new inmate. Until he'd learned how to defend himself.

Right now, all he could feel was the tight headache in his skull and a dull warmth from his foot, probably from where he'd stretched up to get a good angle on the light.

"My arms," Benny said. "I couldn't hold them up anymore."

"You did very well, young man," said Charles. "I've not seen bravery like it."

Seen.

It made them all look at each other briefly, and then turn and look up at the light socket above them. It was the first time Benny realised they could see each other.

The screwdriver was up there, hanging from the black wire. The copper strands had been wrapped around the tool's metal shaft and the flat end was jammed tightly through a hole in the bulb contact. Benny shook his head. He'd made the connection again.

"Christ, that was something Benny," said Giles. "Is it going to be okay up there?"

"The connection will be sound," he replied, still rubbing his head. "But I don't suggest anyone tries the S.O.S. trick again. It was impossible to make a permanent connection. I don't think the screwdriver will stick if we pull it out again. I'm certainly not going to try."

He watched the three of them nod, though there was the same grief he was feeling written all over their faces.

The S.O.S. had been their last chance. Who knows if anyone would have picked it up. He'd only been able to keep it up for a minute or two before his arms collapsed. Who knows if there was *anyone* there to see the signal, anyway. Benny doubted it had even been worth the effort, but surely something was better than nothing.

Benny knew how to accept his situation. He'd done it before. First, the ironic belief that this is all a mistake, that you'll be out of here any time now. Just wait for the door knock. Then the fear part: shit, is this really real? I'm stuck here? Then the anger. How stupid, stupid, stupid, I can't cope with this. Then acceptance. I'm here, and I'm not going anwhere else. Not for a long time. Better get used to it, or go crazy.

"Are you sure you're alright?" said Megan, this time with more emphasis. It caused Benny to come out of his darker thoughts.

Benny saw her eyes flick to Giles' and then down at his feet, and he followed to where they were looking.

On his left foot was Benny's boot, scuffed and dirty, but with leather support running up and over his ankle. But his right foot, no boot this time - he'd used it to hammer the screwdriver - was so bent over to the inside that his ankle seemed to poke outwards. Benny stared at his twisted foot for what felt like a minute. And then his ankle started to hurt.

Really, really hurt.

19

Something was broken, that was for sure.

Benny had rocked on his backside for five minutes, trying to put pressure on his right leg, before he'd finally allowed Megan to look at his ankle.

Not that she knew first aid or anything. She wouldn't know what to do with a broken little finger. But once Benny had seen the awkward angle at which his foot was bent, it quickly became the only sensation he could feel.

He described the agony: the sensation was pure, pulsating pain. Getting worse and worse for every moment he tried to pretend it wasn't there. The pulses of agony spread from his ankle, up his calf muscles until it felt like his whole leg, and then even his whole body ached and throbbed from the pain.

Megan insisted she had a look; she might be able to ease the pressure on his twisted foot. Giles hung around murmuring what he must have thought sounded like positive and reassuring noises, but to Megan his unhelpful loitering made Giles seem to her like an annoying fly that needed to be swatted.

Thankfully, once he found he was not required or even wanted in the first aid tent, Giles seemed happy to turn his attention elsewhere. He made his way back up past Charles, sat down and lit a cigarette.

Benny's foot was turned at an angle. He could keep his leg relatively straight, but his right foot was bent inwards. Megan took a sharp intake of breath as she saw the twist from a different angle.

"I'm going to take your sock off, Benny."

"No, it's okay. I think its just sprained." Megan watched him swallow back the pain, and try to twist his leg a little. He cried out as he did so, only able to put the foot back down exactly as it had been.

Megan shook her head.

"It's definitely worse than sprained," she said with a mix of care and chastisement. Dad would have said to get on with it. Pull your socks up. I can always break the other one, then they'll match. Ha ha ha.

"I think we should take a closer look," said Megan.

Benny grumbled some more but after a moment, relented by pulling up the shins of his grubby jeans to expose the top of a filthy, thick woollen sock.

"I'm sorry," he said, trying to smile. "It's just, these are work socks. They sweat in these boots."

"A sweaty foot is the least of our worries down here," said Megan smiling. Giles puffed smoke into the air, waving his cigarette around.

They all looked around them. Benny's abandoned boot was just the latest of the detritus now scattered around the little curve of the spiral that had too quickly come to feel like ground zero.

Their space.

Home?

The group lingered on the thought a moment too long. Long enough for Megan to register the stink wafting from below them, from another curve in the staircase further down. The family toilet. Giles turned away again, as if searching for an alternative thought.

Quickly, Megan turned back to Benny's leg, rolling down the black wool. She started off tentatively, with just the tips of her fingers, but then with more conviction. As she eased it down, she couldn't help but like the way the soft brown hairs on his shins tickled her fingers. With the pads of her fingers, she could feel strong, taut muscles deeper underneath his smooth skin.

She continued to roll the long woollen sock with one hand, but reached around to cup the back of Benny's leg with the other. The pretext was of needing a firmer grip to keep removing the sock.

For the slightest of moments, she felt she was undressing the man, gently, one piece of clothing at a time. She heard Benny's breathing and when she looked up she saw in his face a smile that was a mix of satisfaction, gratefulness for her tenderness and - maybe she just imagined - the slightest inkling of pleasure.

If it was, it didn't last for long. Megan had drawn the sock down as far as the ankle and could see the red swelling at his ankle pulsating above the top edge.

Forgetting herself for a moment, she attempted to lift Benny's leg so she could slip the sock off over the swollen heel and leg. But the lifting pressure, immediately so abrupt after the gentle finger massage, caused Benny to flinch. She immediately stopped lifting, jumping away from his leg as if the touch of his skin was red hot.

"It's okay," said Benny, heavily blowing air out of his lungs, "just a shock."

Megan connected with his leg once more, wrapping her hand around the back of his calf. She looked up to find Giles, but his attention was concentrated on the roof where Benny had made the electrical connection. She stroked the back of Benny's leg again, with her palm this time, more forcefully and unmistakably in an attempt at a soothing massage. It was hardly an attempt at foreplay, barely sexual at all, but it was tender.

Benny's breathing deepened again. The massage was obviously helping with the pain or, Megan allowed herself to hope, distracting him from it. She looked up and momentarily their eyes connected.

The man smiled gently and in unmistakable assent. She massaged a little deeper, bringing her other hand around the back of his leg too and deepening her grip, moving and pressing and squeezing his calf muscles firmly.

She liked the feel of him and allowed herself the thought of taut, stronger muscles further up his leg. His arms, his shoulders, his chest, his stomach. Benny was a fit man. Not like he's just stepped out of a gym gripping a bottle of whey milkshake. He wasn't like those half-naked fire-fighters Megan had seen on calendars and Facebook shares, all baby oil and flexing.

This was natural strength. She could tell that even with his clothes on. Not exaggerated in any particular place, just strong all over. The natural result of working day after day with heavy materials, lifting and moving. A good body, honestly earned. And all the better for it.

"How's it all going?" Giles' voice interrupted Megan's imagination, his gaze turning her own attention back to the sock. Benny seemed to start at the voice too - perhaps Megan kidded herself, lost in similar appreciation of her body.

She adjusted her neckline, so Giles didn't have such a direct view down her blouse. He'd been snatching views of her cleavage since they got stuck down here.

In half-a-second, Megan and Benny were back fully concentrated on his twisted foot.

"Okay, after three," she said to him calmly, but with a tone that aimed to inspire solidarity.

Benny nodded and placed both of his hands under his thigh, ready to lift. Megan counted down and Benny used his arm strength to lift the dead weight of his right leg. The pain that had dissipated from Megan's tender touch immediately returned, pushing waves of agony from his ankle and into every bone and muscle in his leg. The pain spread into his pelvis which, Benny now realised, must have taken a hit when he'd fallen too.

Benny's lifting gave Megan half an inch to work with. Benny screeched out as she stretched the rolled up edge of the sock over his ankle and flipped it around his swollen heel. With a final deep breath, Benny lowered his leg back to the ground, allowing his foot to roll back into its twisted position. Then, thankfully with a painless movement, Megan flicked the sock off the end of Benny's foot and onto the step below.

The ankle was clearly the problem. The skin around it was deep purple against Benny's black skin, with blood visibly pulsating into the area around his ankle bones. The sight of it caused Megan to look away for a moment. Benny clenched his teeth together as if the sight of the damage alone had doubled the intensity of the pain it was causing.

Giles came down now too, to take a closer look. But he stayed feet away, apparently coy at witnessing such serious injury so up close and personal.

"Ooh, that does not look good," he said, trying to fill the

silence. The other two looked up at him as if his words were the last thing anyone needed to hear.

"Give me a wheeze on that fag," Benny said.

Giles passed it over. Benny took a deep draw on the cigarette, before passing it back.

Benny bent at his spine, leaning over to use his fingers to feel parts of his ankle, trying to locate a single point in the pain which made his whole lower leg feel as if it was on fire. Everything hurt, but the outside join, the place where the ball of the ankle connected with the foot, was incredibly tender.

Through the surrounding skin, Benny's fingertips continued to search until they stopped and began rocking forward and backwards on a particular spot. The faint grinding of bone against bone was audible.

"I think the bone there has splintered or at least fractured. It feels cracked. I need to support it."

Benny was obviously in pain with every rock of his fingers on the joint, but locating the key problem seemed to help him assess the worst of the damage.

"Can you help me lift my leg again?" he asked Megan. She nodded and counted three, before lifting his calf.

"No, I need it higher up," said Benny, speaking through clenched teeth and shaking his head. "Giles?"

The man came down, and Benny asked him to lift his leg again, at the thigh, with both his hands. Megan lifted his leg at the calf. It gave Benny just enough room to...

Megan couldn't believe he was doing it. Benny leaned over his own lifted leg and used his hands to move his twisted foot. He grasped the outside of his foot, pulled the whole limb as close to straight in line with his leg as he could.

He cried out and pushed again, beads of sweat building

on his forehead. Slowly, and obviously against its own will, the foot began to move until Megan saw it click back into place.

The moment the click happened, Benny shouted "'drop". Giles and Megan let go, and Benny's heel hit the ground as he screeched out in pain. But the weight of his leg kept his foot straight, pointing roughly in line with his knee and shin bone.

Benny let out an enormous exhausted sigh, and they all looked down at his foot again. There was definitely something broken in there, but now at least the stretched tendons and other bones were no longer under pressure. They'd heal.

"Jesus Christ, you are some bad motherfucker," said Giles. It was the stuff of movies. Megan couldn't help but nod in agreement, and Charles shook his head in wonder.

The guy had just twisted his own broken and twisted ankle back straight again. Through short, tired breaths, he called to Giles: "Pass me your tie, will you?"

They all waited for a quip from the man about where he'd got the tie, or who made it. But Giles passed it down without comment.

Megan helped Benny lift his leg again, this time just enough for her to slip the edge of the tie underneath his heel. Benny took over then, pulling it taut, then tying it together in an angry knot that forced him to cry out again. There was just enough material remaining to tie it again.

Benny wasn't going anywhere quickly, that was for sure. But the makeshift bandage provided some support and relief. It would allow the swelling around his ankle to form in the right place, rather than between broken bones and stretched tendons. If they ever got out of here, his foot might eventually repair itself in something like the right places.

Benny's breathing relaxed, and he bent his head into his folded arms, too tired to do anything more.

"Let me check the rest of your foot," Megan said with just enough meaning for Benny to pick up the signal, but flat enough that Giles remained oblivious. She gently brought her fingers to Benny's skin, prodding his foot gently, holding here, stroking there.

Only when she knew Giles had turned away again to sit on a step further up, did her efficient and gentle checking transform into a gentle foot massage. Benny lifted one of his arms and rested it gently on Megan's shoulder for a moment. A silent thanks. Something a little more.

Then Benny lifted his head and moved his whole body backwards against the steps, his neck resting comfortably against one. Just enough comfort for him to drift off.

20

When Benny came around, an hour later, Giles seemed impatient to begin the S.O.S. again.

In fact, Charles felt like Giles was impatient about everything. Rude, and brash, and ill mouthed. Like the boys in his A-level classes. Just didn't know when to shut up.

The three younger people did the bashing, with Benny's arms clearly hurting with each bash of his loose boot.

S.O.S., S.O.S.

Charles didn't have the puff. He was still heavy breathing from having to tread down and then up from the bathroom area that morning. Benny hadn't been able to accompany him, of course. Sweet as she was to offer, it hadn't seemed appropriate for Megan to go.

"Come on then, Charlie Boy," said Giles. "I'll help you down, but I'm not sticking around for the action. You can call me when you're done."

When Charles had recovered from the effort of his toilet visit, he spoke.

"I might suggest, we write a letter? Or several letters,

perhaps? We might write them, then leave them as far up the stairs as we can."

"*We* can?" said Giles. "Seems that's just me and Megan now."

"We can all write them, though," he said. "And then, if you would be so kind…"

"Sure, Charlie Boy. I am forever your humble servant."

Charles was bored with Giles. Just like the boys on the back row at school, taking every opportunity to have a poke at him. As if he couldn't understand the meaning behind their gestures. The disrespect they showed him by flinging balls of paper around the room whenever he turned his back.

The young man thought he was so funny. So above everyone else. But he was nothing more than the show-off bullies in each of his history classes, from the day he started teaching to the day he left his last job.

Revise that. There were idiots like Giles in the Navy, too. Attention seekers. Time wasters. They thought they'd make life easier for everyone cooped up in the tiny spaces of the submarines by playing the fool. Really, it made most others miserable.

And that same behaviour was getting on his nerves right now, even though they all had far more space to move around. Giles you're a fool. And the worst thing is, you don't know it. But sometime soon, you're going to learn one huge lesson.

"Well, I'm going to write my letters," said Charles. "In case there is someone up there. In case I die. In case of, well, whatever."

He pulled out his notebook. "Anyone want a page, just ask."

Charles didn't bother to start a letter asking for rescue. Rescue was about science. Or in this case, the lack of it.

Science said there should be a top of this staircase. Science said there should be a bottom. Science said there should be other people going up and down.

Maybe this was philosophy. The actual fact that he was thinking about this at all proved he was alive, at least in some form or other. *I think therefore I am.* The most important statement in modern philosophy. Thank you Descartes.

Only, you can play with philosophy. You can imagine universes existing underneath your fingernails. You ask which way an arrow is pointing, and challenge others to explain why without the use of another arrow.

But that's all theoretical stuff.

As far as Charles was concerned, his situation was real, whatever the philosophy.

His chest hurt, despite the odd tablet he'd taken. His throat was dry and sore. He went into a painful coughing fit every ten minutes. He had no energy left.

He felt the deep sadness of loneliness, more painful than all the other hurts put together.

There would be no rescue here. Only Sickness Unto Death. He shook his head as he tried to remember which philosopher had written that book.

No, in his letter, he would write history. His own. Putting out *his* truth.

It would be no famous letter, with infamous outcome.

He was no Charles Darwin, writing to a colleague, outlining his first theories on evolution.

His would not be the letter received by Lord Monteagle

in October 1605, that could have prevented Guy Fawkes and the Gunpowder Plot getting as far as it did.

Nikita Khrushchev's letters to J.F. Kennedy during The Cuban Missile Crisis narrowly avoiding a third world war.

Even Jack the Ripper sent taunting letters to the police on the hunt for him.

Charles shook his head again. Jack the Ripper had carried out his ugly campaign only a stone's throw from where they were now.

Strong powerful letters, that in their own way changed the world. His could be nothing of their weight or importance.

But perhaps his letter could bring closure for him.

'*My dear Felicity,*' he began.

21

"Who's that guy on the TV?" asked Giles.

"Is this a game, to pass the time," said Megan. "Because that's a pretty wide category."

Giles could hear a rasp in her voice. The same one he'd heard from everyone that morning. Like dust had settled permanently in everyone's throats, and swallowing felt like dragging his tonsils along sandpaper. Everyone was wetting their lips frequently.

Giles coughed.

"No, that guy who goes to the forests and stuff. Eats grubs."

"Bear Grylls," said Benny.

"Yeah, Bear Grylls," said Giles. "I saw a programme of his, in the desert probably. He talked about how to make water and food, when there's nothing else about."

"Let me guess, cactuses and squeezing lizards guts?"

"I think that would be cacti," said Charles.

"Cheers, brain box. So..."

"I don't see no cacti. Nor lizards," said Benny.

"What about rats?" said Giles.

"That's disgusting," said Megan.

"Not as disgusting as dying here, sitting in our own shit."

"Okay, Giles, but I don't see no rats neither. Let alone a way to cook one."

Giles thought of his lighter.

What you going to do, set light to your jacket and spit roast a rat? Wasting your time. Better off you and the big man spit roasting...

Giles shut off the voices before they finished. Idiots.

"Just a thought. We might find, I don't know, later on. Down at the number two station, some interest from some furry friends."

"Wow, this is desperate," said Megan.

"And I'm getting desperate to eat," shouted Giles.

Easy, don't want to scare the horses. Keep her on side.

"I'm not eating rat," said Megan. "Nor mice."

Not desperate enough yet, Giles. Give her another day, maybe two. She'll gnaw off her own arm.

Benny spoke: "I have seen no rodents, not up here, not down there. But if you catch one Giles, I sure as hell would do my best to skin it."

"It's the fleas they carry that are dangerous," said Giles, smiling.

"Enough!" shouted Megan.

"Okay, sweetheart. Your turn?"

"What does Bear Grylls say about water, again?"

"In extreme circumstances?"

"I'd call this extreme," she said.

Everyone knew.

Go on, say it. Be the filthy one.

"You drink your own piss."

"Ah, Jesus..." said Benny.

"No, really. I reckon Charles would back me up here. Won't you Charlie Boy?"

Charles nodded. Giles still felt it was a reluctant concession.

"On the subs..."

"Yes, yes, Charlie Boy, on the subs."

Charles went quiet. Megan scowled at him.

Giles filled the silence: "I don't know it for certain, but I'm sure Bear Grylls drinks his own piss on the TV. Stands to reason. You drink a lot, you piss a lot."

And when you're out on the beers Giles, you piss an awful lot. Including up walls, into people's gardens, down back alleys. We all do. What a waste. Should have reserved it for down here.

"I reckon 60 or 70 percent of your piss is just water."

"I can't believe we're even talking about this," said Megan.

"Ah, don't be so precious, sweetheart. You know you've been thinking about it. We all have," Giles snapped back.

"The problem is the rest," said Charles, finally speaking up.

"What's that Charles?" asked Benny.

"The rest. The 20 or 30 percent that's not water. It's toxic. It's what your body doesn't want. We learned it in the Navy,"

"Of course," said Giles.

"Yes, the Navy. You can drink your own urine. But only little bits at a time. And only for a short time. Otherwise the toxicity builds up."

"Hold on," said Benny. "You saying, we can drink our own urine?"

"I'm not sure I've got any left," said Megan.

"Yes," said Charles. "Some ancient civilisations did it, as part of rituals. I wouldn't advise it."

"But little sips? If we're absolutely desperate?" said Giles.

You remember, don't you Giles? At Uni. To get into the Borat Club? Ten pints, then a shot of your own piss. Then on for a vindaloo. You became a Boratee, didn't you, Giles? You pulled that night, too. Didn't tell her about the piss though.

"Well, I'm not that desperate yet," said Megan.

"Better save up for when you are, though," said Giles. He waved his empty Lucozade bottle.

"Anyone else got any containers?"

"I'm not drinking your piss," said Benny.

"I'm not offering."

Giles watched as each of the other three subtly looked around. Benny had his little toolbag, Charlie Boy rifled through his pockets, Megan looked briefly in her purse.

"Can you eat lipstick?" she said.

"You can write messages with it," said Benny.

"Good idea," Megan said.

"And use the cap to collect your wee," said Giles.

Giles felt the discussion had broken through, and now created a lighter-hearted atmosphere. He was pleased he'd been at the centre, without a drop of booze in his blood. Without a lear or disgusting insinuation or a double entendre. He could be funny without being extreme. He even felt sorry he'd put Charles down.

See guys, I don't need you.

"You see that CV," Giles attempted, pointing towards Megan's side.

"One single page, not very impressive," she said, smiling for once at him.

"Do you know how to make one of those origami cups?"

They all smiled again.

"If you do, you're all welcome to use it. Though I get first dibs if it really comes to it. Worth more than the qualifications written on it, at least," said Megan.

Everyone smiled.

"Meanwhile, I'm going upstairs with this lipstick. What should I write?"

22

Megan decided to climb further up the spiral staircase than anyone had gone before. Was it 300 steps Giles had climbed?

She left her shoes with the group. She'd do 50 steps at a time, then take a rest. There was nothing else to do, and she was missing doing any exercise. Though she felt like her skin and muscles were already hanging off her bones, and she had no energy for anything at all.

But she was bored, and realised the lipstick might be a good way to get any attention if anyone was up there. She was still a believer, even now, that they'd be rescued. That this was some weird accident. If they did nothing, it was admitting defeat. She started counting her steps, marking every 50 with a slash of lipstick on a tile by the bannister.

Megan hadn't noticed Rachel until her classmate had spoken to her first. The two of them were left in the class-room after a lecture on marketing pyramids. It had been so boring and obvious that even the lecturer seemed to leap out of the class at the end to escape it.

"I just don't understand this," Rachel said from behind

Megan, with a little despair in her voice. She was about three desks back from Megan, who was sitting at the front, trying to squeeze out any bit of knowledge that the incompetent lecturer offered. The girl spoke so quietly she might have been at the back of the class.

Megan looked around, checking the thin, quiet girl was talking to her and not to herself.

"Oh, I think it's quite obvious once you get it," said Megan in a superior tone, turning properly to face the girl. "Spread the word to a few people with quality leads, they spread the word to others, and boom-boom-boom, suddenly you're Microsoft." She smiled.

The girl looked up from her desk, her eyes a little distant.

"That's what I mean," she whispered, releasing a little sigh and the tinniest shake of her head. "I don't understand why we're here being taught any old thing you could come up with yourself in five minutes, and look up on the internet in two.

There's a whole bunch of YouTube marketing videos. I must have watched them all and every one gave you more information, and in a far more interesting way, than the last 45 minutes."

The girl ducked her head again and started packing up her stuff, as if she was embarrassed about letting her guard down.

"I know exactly what you mean," said Megan gently, without the sarcasm of the last time she spoke. The girl wasn't just mouthing off. She sounded resigned and disappointed.

"I guess they have to aim it at the lowest level to, well to include everyone."

Megan knew how the girl felt. Every day she turned up,

hoping today would be the day when she actually learned some new information. Something that would help propel her to the dizzy heights of business and the City. Every day she'd go home feeling every hour she'd spent at college was another wasted. Everything lacked substance and ambition. Maybe Dad was right.

"Ah well," the girl said. "I guess I'll see you tomorrow."

"I'm Megan." A questioning tone that only gently expected a reply.

"Yes, I know. Nice to meet you..." the girl dropped her gaze, and waved her hands as if to take in the whole class-room and the last two months all in one gesture, "properly."

The girl stood up and and made for the door.

"I'm Rachel," she said. Then she was gone.

Megan realised Rachel had been there every day, too. Usually early into class like she was, always with her head buried in the work. She'd seen her in the library, at a particular table in the corner that overlooked the only green space in the college. A little square of lawn with what passed for a modern art sculpture plonked in the middle.

But the two had never made eye-contact. She was just an inconspicuous face, invisible among the much larger and far louder characters in the class.

Rachel never asked questions, never volunteered answers either. Megan was sociable with her classmates, at least on the surface. It was the only way she could get through the day.

Rachel appeared to have made a conscious effort not to do so, to make herself invisible. Everything about her said she didn't want to be there. She didn't seem to fit in. Like she'd ended up there by accident.

For a week or two, Rachel became invisible again. Megan

tried a few times to start conversations, but it was hard to break through small talk.

'How are you?' And 'Nice weekend?' only goes so far if the person you're asking only offers 'Fine, thanks' and 'Not much, really,' in response.

With the other girls, such questions generated a lengthy rendition about shopping trips and nights out and pubs and boyfriends and hairdos and holidays, which wasn't what Megan wanted either.

But slowly Megan and Rachel began to smile at each other as they came into class. They continued to be the first ones to take their seats. They graduated to sharing raised eyebrows or a subtle shake of the head as a tutor would state something like the importance of good spelling when writing letters and emails, or learning to touch type rather than stabbing at the keys. What next, dress well for an interview?

Megan couldn't remember when the two had started speaking properly, but a few times she'd sat by Rachel as they both worked overlooking the square.

She began sitting next to Rachel on the concrete bench outside the college - "do you mind if I?" - to eat their M&S sandwiches. After a chicken wrap one day, Megan could stand the distance no more. Rachel was obviously a kindred spirit. She asked asked her if she'd like to join her for a cup of muddy coffee the dispenser churned out in the college canteen.

Rachel didn't talk much, and kept the conversation formal, talking about the work and the tutors.

But that was okay. Megan had plenty of talk for the two of them. Megan talked about her dad and how he didn't understand why she wanted to work hard instead of taking the easy option.

She talked about the other girls in the class, sharing bits and pieces of gossip to fill the spaces in the conversation. She talked about the tutors, how they were useless and the two of them together probably already knew everything they were going to learn on this course.

Rachel didn't share much. She had an ordinary family in Chigwell, with whom she still lived, and didn't seem to have any ambition to leave. She led a normal life, studying and reading the papers on the weekend. School didn't work out for me, she said. She didn't have a boyfriend - nor a girlfriend, Megan learned after a little more prodding - and it didn't seem to bother her.

One day, over a punnet of tuna and pasta salad, Megan had declared to Rachel that it was her towering ambition to get out of Essex and to work in some high powered City job.

Perhaps she should just get on with applying for jobs instead of being held back by this crappy college. She'd been dealt a raw deal in life, stuck on this course. She'd have to fight harder than most to get what she wanted, but nothing was going to hold her back.

"I don't belong here," she said with a mouth full of pasta. "You don't belong here either, Rachel. What the hell are we both doing here?"

She saw Rachel's eyes well up before she ducked her head, excused herself, and headed into the building and towards the toilets. When she returned, the redness in her eyes had gone, and she picked up her salad without a word.

"Sorry, Rachel, did I say something..."

"No, no," said Rachel. "Just having a bad day."

"Ah, boy trouble or something?" Megan desperately wanted in on her friend's life. They were becoming friends, weren't they?

"Yeah, something like that," Rachel replied. But the salad

was finished. It was time to go back to class. Megan took Rachel's punnet into hers, and threw them both into the bin at the edge of the square.

———

At four hundred steps up, Megan decided she'd gone far enough. She'd marked seven lipstick marks on her way up, and now it was time to write something.

HELP!

Four people stranded.

Hungry. Thirsty.

400 steps down.

PLEASE!

Reluctantly she wrote her Dad's phone number.

He'd be worried sick. No, not worried.

Angry.

Many times, he'd accused her of using *his* house like a hotel. If she came back late. If she didn't bring back any shopping. If she didn't call when she was away for longer than he expected.

God forbid, if she stayed the night with a boy.

If she did anything he couldn't control. He wouldn't let her even consider buying or renting her own place, and refused to guarantee a mortgage for her.

For a moment she considered scribbling out Dad's number. But whose number would she write?

Did she have any real friends? Or just acquaintances. Dad had stood in the way of her getting to know anyone well enough for her to memorise their phone number. The rest were just names on her mobile. Long out of battery. Not worth being in touch with, anyway.

Megan sat on the 400th step. For the first time, she was

properly away from the other three. For a moment, she allowed a rising feeling of claustrophobia. The bin again.

No.

If there was one thing she was going to defeat down here, it was that. There was no choice. She'd push it away, take charge, like she'd taken charge of her career.

And when she got out of here - and she *was* going to get out of here - she'd go right to Rank and Tudor and slam her revised CV down on the desk of the CEO.

She'd demand a decent job that reflected her talents, her hard work. And the massive achievement of surviving being buried alive for, what was it now, 36 hours?

"Fuck you, Dad."

She shivered. Considered herself. Her head hurt with the dehydration, her throat was dry.

Her whole body ached from the climbing, but also from sleeping awkwardly, and not being replenished.

She had a period of feeling dizzy yesterday, as her brain came to terms with sustenance shortage. Now her whole body just felt full of dry sand. She felt she could sleep anywhere. Any time. In any place. Her skin was flaky. Her toes and fingers were losing feeling.

The body shuts down, she thought, to protect itself. The brain in particular. A kind of hibernation, she imagined.

She should have stuffed herself with pizza and donuts and bagels before coming down here, like a hedgehog overeats bugs and worms before going into a deep sleep over the winter.

Weird thoughts.

Was that part of the slow process of dying from hunger?

She needed to drink. Desperately.

She pulled out a small perfume pump spray bottle from

her bra. She'd kept it hidden from the others. Dad had given it to her.

No, that wouldn't work. She replaced it.

She looked at her lipstick, now worn down to practically nothing. She looked at the lid. Maybe an inch of canister. Things had got that desperate.

She couldn't believe she was about to do this. She hitched up her skirt and hoped desperately that Giles hadn't followed her up.

23

Megan woke up, needing to pee again. She also needed a drink, though she kept that quiet. She was embarrassed and disgusted by what she'd done the afternoon before.

She'd kept it quiet, while Giles had boasted about pissing into his Lucozade bottle. He'd sipped it in front of everyone, scrunched his face with the taste, and then pretended it was okay, really.

"Not quite your Chardonnay," he'd said. "But better than the piss they served in my local."

Grinning, he had offered it up to Benny, then down to Megan and Charles. Both had passed. Charles had become quiet in the evening, no longer really engaging with the group. She'd seen him become paler and his eye sockets withdrawn.

Giles was still asleep, as far as she could tell. Benny was staring into space. Of all of them he always seemed the most comfortable.

Megan edged down the steps, taking care to keep to the

centre of the staircase so she didn't wake Charles as she passed.

She took a few more steps, then leaped back and released a shrill scream. Somewhere between a deep intake of breath and a screech. Beneath it, the unmistakable sound of disgust.

"Oh, fuck," she said, backing up the stairs. "Oh God Benny, oh God. He's white; no he's blue. Oh, God."

She started retching, bent over and heaving. Her back convulsed as she wrapped an arm around her stomach. But there was nothing to come out. She was crying uncontrollably.

"Oh fuck," she said. "Fuck, fuck, no, no." She started to kick the wall, flail out, grabbing the back of her head, and pulling into her chest, wildly rocking from side to side.

"Benny, Benny," she shouted.

"It's okay," the man said, trying to get up from where he was.

But it wasn't going to be okay. Megan was sure of that now as she kicked the steps and resisted the temptation to bang her head against the hard tiles.

She knew it right through to her aching bones and her bruised toes. It wasn't going to be okay at all.

And the reason it wasn't going to be okay was that Charles was dead. She tried to push the thought away, but it kept creeping back in.

Charles was the first to die.

It wasn't the first time Benny had seen a dead body. Not by a long shot. He'd seen a few drug overdoses. Someone was shot dead by a fellow robber at a jeweller's shop they'd raided. Another time, after a party at his slate, someone just never woke up.

He hadn't ever killed anyone himself, though he'd roughed a few up. But with the drug overdoses, the fucked-up robbery, he'd been there. That was just as bad.

Benny hauled himself up from his sitting position, using the handrail for support. Clearly, Giles would do nothing. And Megan was panicking so much she was incapable.

In agony, he lifted his leg, and used his stronger one and the handrail to hop down, past Giles, to where Charles was lying. Megan seemed to calm with his presence. She placed her hand on Benny's back, rubbed it a little, then went up some steps to weep.

Benny knew nothing about taking a pulse, but it didn't take more than a moment when he came level with Charles to know it wouldn't be necessary.

The guy's eyes were closed. His face and hands were as dull grey as the tiles above the bannister. His lips were a haunting muddy blue, deeper at the edges. It had happened in his sleep.

The lucky bastard hadn't even known about it.

Giles and Megan watched. Benny steeled himself as he kneeled down and reached out to touch the body, which was sprawled out. The side of him felt hard to the touch. It rocked slightly as Benny pushed him with his hands, as if he was trying to wake him.

Poor guy.

More confident now, Benny ran his hands down Charles' jacket and felt a weight in the pocket. He pushed his hands inside and brought out a small leather notebook, then returned to retrieve a small dark canister. He shook it, then flipped the top and peered inside at a dozen tiny white pills.

He looked up at the other two, then placed them back in Charles' pocket.

He opened the notebook, then shifted around painfully to sit on the narrowing step by Charles' side. He glanced over the pages, scanning neat handwriting detailing ships and spices, countries and dates. Benny remembered what Charles had said yesterday: *This is me. It's my private work. It's all I have.*

He flicked to the last pages he'd written on.

'My dear Felicity,'

He closed the book and leaned over, placed it back in Charles' blazer pocket. He knew Charles would probably have a wallet in the other pocket, but that was enough. What was his was his. Any photographs or memories left would go with him.

Megan turned to Benny, who was still sitting below him. "I don't know how much more I can take of this. I can't look at him."

She pointed at Charles. "He's the lucky one, he's out of this. But I can't sit here next to his body."

"I'll take him down. Past the toilet area. Giles will help."

Giles stood, reluctant, Benny thought.

"Don't leave me alone," she cried.

"You'll be fine. We'll carry Charles down and come right back up."

"I can't bear it," she said. "Oh, fuck, this is just the worst."

"Calm down, Meg," said Giles. "It's one less person to worry about."

"Fuck off, Giles."

Benny watched him smile.

"Help me, you fool," he said.

"Should we, say a prayer, or something?" Megan said.

Benny thought of the Chaplain at the Programme.

I'm always here if you want to talk. God wants to hear you talk.

God had done nothing for Benny. God was doing nothing for them down here in this hole. God had been wholly absent his entire life.

"No, we shouldn't," he said, a tightness in his voice. Then softer. "We know nothing about Charles, whether he believed."

Benny stood again, using the bannister as support. Giles joined him.

"Megan, we're going to have to drag him down. I suggest you go for a walk."

Megan nodded through tears. Turned, and made her way up steps and out of view.

"Put your hands under his shoulders," said Benny. "Don't let his head bang off the steps. We can give him that at least."

Giles did as he was told, though he turned his head away as he grasped Charles' jacket. Benny began hauling the dead man down the steps. The man wasn't particularly heavy, and gravity did its job, as the stiff body worked its way down the spiral, with Benny hopping down on one leg.

They'd rest for a moment or two, then heave again. Neither wanted to wait too long for fear of realising what they were actually doing.

They pulled Charles down past the two toilet areas, both of them scrunching their eyes at the stink. At the number two area, Benny insisted they both lift the man, so he didn't have to be dragged through their waste.

Giles did his best, Benny thought, but he had to use his own strength to do most of the work, despite the sheering pain in his ankle when he was forced to put pressure on it. At least his foot stayed in its socket.

Finally, they agreed he was far enough down. Benny dropped Charles' legs, and Giles gently lowered the man's head onto a step. Despite his pale skin, Charles looked like he was sleeping. Half an hour ago, everyone had thought he had been.

Benny pulled out Charles' hankie, the one from his top pocket, and laid it across the man's face

They both stood there in silence.

Giles was okay. Benny could see how the guy could be obnoxious, and he'd noticed the slight tics the man had, his tendency to be cruel, but he was no worse than some of the other suits he'd see on the Tube late at night.

Lots of talk, but no action. God, he'd seen far more creepy guys with far more power. Down here, everyone was vulnerable. Giles was scared and confused, and that could come out as a little crazy.

As their bodies ran out of food and water, weren't they all going a bit nuts? He'd seen some stuff, and they were nowhere near that yet.

We just need to keep clear heads. He thought of Stevie.

"As long as we can keep our heads clear, Giles, we'll get through this, you'll see."

Slowly the two climbed the steps to Megan, who had returned to her step. They took their own places and sat to look where Charles had been.

They sat in silence for an hour. It might have been two.

24

"So, how long was it we can go without food or water?"

It wasn't a question Giles wanted to ask, but the gnawing emptiness in his stomach, combined with the dry gritty pain that accompanied every swallow, forced him to break the silence. He was sure every one of them was thinking the same right now.

He'd already started drinking his own urine, but it didn't make him any less thirsty.

There was a general ache across his whole body. It felt like his brain was drying out like a sponge left out in the sun. Any liquid or cushioning in his skull had long since drained away.

"Isn't it five days without food, and eight days without water?" Megan said. "Or, is it the other way around?"

Benny stared down at the ground, tracing circles into the ground with his fingertip. As if he was trying to ignore the question.

"Well, however long it is, we haven't got any of either. My head is hurting like crazy and my throat is so parched I can hardly speak. Don't we have anything between us?"

"I'd go for a steak right now," said Megan. "Medium rare, with the fat leaking into the chips. A huge pint of lager. No girly glasses. I mean a pint, a huge pint." She mimicked pouring the beer into her throat in one greedy gesture. Once she'd finished the imaginary pint, she sighed with a satisfied smile.

Giles loved the vision, and even Benny looked up from the floor.

"One of those big German steins of beer for me," said Giles, holding up both of his hands as if carrying and swinging a two-litre jug in each one. "Here's your weiss-beer, and your bratvurst will be along in just a few minutes."

It was an awful German accent, but both Benny and Megan smiled at Giles' attempt. The atmosphere became almost jovial, and Giles was glad he'd created a smile in the other two. He wasn't *such* a shit.

Anything to take his mind off the feeling of hard stones rolling around in his stomach.

"And what will it be, Frau Megan?" he continued. "For desert, the Black Forest gateau, or simply a single scoop of ice-cream?"

"The gateau, of course," sighed Megan, looking up at the roof as if the menu was written there. Giles imaged a thick and creamy chocolate cake. He could almost taste the cherries.

"Ah, of course Frau Megan. A little 1980s, but a slice of Black Forest gateau it is."

"With cream."

"Jawohl, with cream naturally, for your slice and for Herr Benny?"

Benny could hold his stony face no longer.

"Sod the cream," he said. For a second or two his voice

sounded genuinely angry. "Just bring out the whole fucking cake. And three massive spoons."

They all laughed. Genuinely laughed. The chamber echoed with the sound and it felt like it was the first time for two days that they had let their guard down. They allowed the absurdity rather than the nightmare of their situation to take over.

Giles was pleased with how his little skit had gone down. Funny didn't always have to be about *birds with big tits*, or *giving her one* or some smartarse comment about some over-paid footballer. Just shared amusement about a terrible situation they were all in, and not at someone else's expense. It was refreshing.

But Giles allowed the silence after the shared laugh to last a few beats too long. Benny's addition, 'three spoons', hung in the air between them all and reminded them they had once been four.

An awful thought entered Giles' head, but he pushed it away before it properly formed. But reason told him the other two must be thinking the same thing. It was grotesque, but someone now had to say it. And since it was Giles who'd started the whole food conversation in the first place, perhaps it really ought to be him that allowed the thought to escape.

"Do you think that Charles maybe brought anything to eat with him," said Giles, trying to find a tone that bridged between their jovial spirits just now and the seriousness of their true situation. "He was the kind of guy who'd take a packed lunch to the library?"

"Oh Giles," said Megan.

"Or a flask or something," said Giles.

"He didn't have a bag, though," said Benny, revealing he too had been thinking along the same lines. "He didn't turn anything out on the step. And when we took him down, I didn't see or feel anything."

"But you didn't go through his all his pockets?"

"No, Giles, I didn't go through a dead man's pockets. I only picked up his notebook."

"So, maybe - I don't know - maybe he was carrying some sandwiches or something. A chocolate bar?"

Megan recoiled at the thought. "I don't know if I could eat the food from a dead man. And *definitely* not some two-day-old cheese sandwich. Or a mouldy apple."

"It's just food," said Giles.

"Yes, but it's yesterday's food. No, the day before. And it's been squashed against his... his corpse. His body, all this time." She shivered again, sickened at the thought.

"It's not like we have a choice," said Giles despite the rising sickness in his own throat.

"Hold on," Benny interrupted. "Even if he had solid food, well he's down there after the toilet area. If he had a sandwich, not only would it be days old but it probably wouldn't even be safe to eat. Would it?"

Giles snapped. "Safe to eat? Compared with what?" He stood up and waved his hands around the echoing chamber. "Compared with sitting here and dying of hunger? People have done much worse than eating a day old sandwich. People have survived. People have had to... eat each other."

"Giles," Megan said suddenly, cutting him off from the very thought, trying to erase the very notion from her mind. She shook her head and drew her palms across her eyes, weary from the discussion. It had been so much fun a moment ago.

"Look Megan, I can't believe that I'm agreeing with Giles about anything at all, but for once perhaps he has a point.

Charles may have had a snack bar or something. Some well wrapped sandwiches. He was definitely the type.

"I'm not saying I'm going to gobble up whatever he's got, but if he had something edible, non-perishable, I guess I could just about stomach a bit. We won't know unless we try. And the longer we wait to try, well the less edible anything he has is going to be."

Giles watched, surprised by Benny's solidarity.

A point to you Giles. A few more and you might score.

"We're just going to look," Giles said, looking around at the other two as if it was a committee decision. "Then consider our options."

Benny's smile rose again, almost to the level of the humour they'd shared a moment ago.

"What's all this talk of *we*?" he said. Then Benny put on his own poor German accent. "You are ze chef in this restaurant, Herr Giles. We are looking forward to what you will prepare for us?"

Hah, your round Giles. Make mine a double tequila. You wanker.

Giles felt his face go slightly pale with the realisation. Someone was going to have to go down and search the pockets of Charles' corpse, a turn or two down from their own toilet waste.

And he had just volunteered for the job.

The first thing that rose even just a handful of steps down away from where they gathered was the stench. When you desperately needed to go, Giles supposed, you didn't notice the smell so much. Any anyway, then there was little choice but to hold your nose and contribute to the now growing toilet area.

But this was different. The smell was not only so obnoxious as to be unbearable; the stench carried with it a sticky cloyingness that congealed in the throat. It was all-encompassing and impossible. And not only was Giles going past the toilet area and further down, he was going down past all that putrid muck specifically in search of food.

Giles held his single sleeve up to his nose and mouth, and turned away. No, it wasn't worth. He'd rather starve. It wasn't the grumble in his stomach that made him continue, but the sense of embarrassment among the others for not carrying out the search he'd promised.

Do it! Do it! Do it! All the way Giles. Drink! Drink! Drink! Hooray!

Giles held his breath and couldn't bear to look as he picked his way through, finding patches of concrete as yet unsullied. Twice he could feel his empty stomach and parched throat retching and had to stare resolutely at the wall for a moment, keeping his whole body still so as not to step in something. How could they have produced so much?

This last thought pushed him on a few last steps until he was clear of it all, the smell slightly relenting again to just a generalised smell of crap and the grime and the sweat all of them had got used to living in. He shook himself down, as a dog shakes off dirty water. The worst was over. All he had to do now was...

Before he'd completed the thought, a light grey mop of hair came into view. Charles.

Giles found the sight of a dead body intriguing rather than disgusting, certainly not as putrid as the scene he had just passed through. When Benny and he had taken the body down earlier, it had been functional. The man had not been real.

But now Giles had to face that Charles had been alive. And now was dead.

Regret.

Was that what he was feeling now?

The hankie Benny had placed across Charles' face had slipped away, leaving the older man exposed. Charles' face was marble white, with traces of blue arteries pressed close to the skin, making his skin look a little like a ripe cheese. But his face was incredibly still. His eyes were tightly closed and, it seemed to Giles, he was entirely expressionless. Charles didn't look ill at ease or in pain, he didn't look satisfied or scared. He didn't even look asleep. He looked vacant, empty. No one home.

Giles waited for some quip to enter his head, an echo of a voice from his crude workmates. Surely they'd have a joke about this situation. But all remained quiet. He was glad.

"Nothing else is out of bounds, boys, however crude. So, why so coy about death? You assholes."

Charles' body remained folded up, the way the two had left him. Standing there above him, Giles felt a momentary jealousy. If death was a long, peaceful, comfortable sleep - away from this place, away from the troubles that could press down onto you like a fallen wall - then maybe Charles was better off.

What had been this man's story? His wife had left him, that much Giles remembered. He'd been sacked from school, and Giles suspected why. But Charles seemed sad. Resigned.

Giles wished he'd listened properly to the man. Given him a chance. It wasn't as if Giles always put his own hands where they were invited: school, work, nightclubs. What was the difference? A no was a no, right? A momentary twisting of Giles' stomach rose from deep inside.

He'd made fun of this guy, and what was he? A puny, defenceless and - admit it - obviously already quite ill man. The old bugger had been an easy target, a plaything for Giles without a chance to defend himself.

And for what? Showing off? Playing top dog? Giles cursed the voices in his head. After all, Giles' and Charles' stories weren't dissimilar.

Giles looked again at the old man's emotionless face. He wanted to reach out and touch. To lay his hand over his forehead. But that felt somehow intrusive. Insensitive. In life, Giles hadn't earned the familiarity to be tender with Charles. And now it was too late.

Instead, he kneeled down to touch the older man's hand. A handshake was what he had in mind, a 'sorry old chap, I've been an idiot, let me buy you a drink'. Not that Giles had ever said anything like to that to someone who was alive.

Is that moths I see coming out of your wallet, Giles?

"Fuck off," Giles whispered.

Giles reached his fingers out gently and rested them on the back of one of Charles' hand. Two fingers, then three. The skin was cold to the touch. Not, as Giles had expected, so cold as if Charles' body has come out of a fridge. Just as hard and lifeless as the tiles and the concrete and the steps all around them both. When you touch other people, they are warm and full of energy, but at the time you never notice it. It was only when you felt the opposite did the sheer aliveness of people become so apparent.

By now, Giles had gently rested the whole of his palm over the back of Charles' still hand. He gently rocked his hand side to side, the closest gesture to a shake.

"For what it's worth, Charles," he whispered. He patted

the old man's hand a few times, almost in a matey way, and tried to lighten the tone of his voice. "Sorry to have to do this to you, old chap."

As he moved to the job in hand, he felt the rise again of slight sickness in his stomach. Giles would have to concentrate if he didn't want the nausea to win over. He patted the old man down over the top of his jacket. First the top breast pocket, which was empty, and then the side pockets. In one of Charles' pockets he felt a rattle and dug tentatively inside to pull out a canister. He popped the lid and looked down on a dozen tiny white tablets. Obviously not recreational. Most likely to be statins or beta-blockers. Something to keep the heart beating and the blood thin.

He bounced the canister in his hand a few times, then without allowing himself too much thought, pocketed the pills. More use upstairs than down here.

In the same pocket he found a small notebook but resisted the temptation to open it and read, remembering that Benny had already done so. He replaced the book back in Charles' pocket.

Giles rolled the man's stiff body over slightly to feel the outside of the man's other jacket pocket, before delving inside to turn out its pockets. A thick wallet with a pass for the British Library, a twenty-pound note and a passport photo of a nondescript older lady that, Giles thought, could have been anyone's mum.

Felicity. He patted the old man's body again, remembering Charles' words in the dark the night before he died. 'She left, I'm alone.'

Some loose change toppled from the pocket and disturbed the silence as a few coins rolled down a step or two. Giles fished inside the pocket again. But apart from a few ancient balls of fluff and a biro, there was nothing there.

He moved to the main's inside jacket pocket, but here was nothing there either. This was a futile exercise. Felicity would have made his packed lunch. Slipped in a snack for Charles for his library visit.

But Felicity was gone. She'd left. That was all.

Tentatively, Giles moved his hands down to the sides of Charles trousers, disturbing the stench of the urine that had stained his trousers. Avoiding the urine, which had barely dried in the staircase's humidity.

Giles felt his left pocket first. Nothing. This was a man who travelled light, not weighed down by all the accoutrements of life that a high intensity supposedly rewarding job in the City offered. Meaningless stuff. Giles' iPad, sitting in his drawer at work was no better for writing than this biro when it got down to it. And a biro didn't need a battery or power source, something decidedly absent down this staircase.

On Charles' left hand, Giles saw the man's wedding ring. A simple gold band. Only some things really mattered. Despite himself, Giles glanced down at his own empty wedding finger. All the rest is just stuff.

In Charles' right trouser pocket, Giles felt a moment of quiet excitement. There he felt a light bulge and the promise of sandwiches or a squashed bun. It wouldn't be very appetising, but it would be something to eat. And more than any of the rest of them had. He fished inside, but pulled out only a damp handkerchief.

Megan had been the one to stop to check if Charles was alright. And hadn't she said she was already late for an interview? She'd promised to stay with him until help came.

There was a time when Giles might have done that. A time long, long ago. He looked down again at Charles' wedding ring. He placed his palm over the dead man's hand again.

He waited for a moment and thought some more. The boys had been relatively quiet down here, in a situation which required meaning, sensitivity, some tact, some consideration. He thought of Lisa and how she had helped him. Calmed the voices. Lifted the depression.

Giles was out of his own medication, but perhaps trying to concentrate on kindness and being thoughtful, maybe that might keep the darkness in check.

He stood and moved back upwards to the others and told them he'd found nothing to eat on Charles' body.

25

The only problem Megan had with Rachel was that she always found college so easy.

After they'd become friends - if that was what they were, Megan was never sure - they would occasionally compare notes. Megan didn't share everything she could have. It was *her* work and she had to really try at it. Just like her GCSEs.

But Rachel seemed to take it all in her stride, showing no obvious stress or desperation, finding it all too easy. And her work always ended up so perfect.

Rachel didn't even *need* to do what Megan did. Rachel always seemed to do everything better. She was more creative with ideas. More instinctive with business. Sharp with the maths. God, she even had neater handwriting.

Megan had to work hard to maintain above average. Rachel was top of the class without blinking. It took little for her to be excellent.

What was she even doing there? She was making Megan look like she belonged with this lot. Those girls dragging their heels into college because there was nothing better to fill their time.

There was only one space at the top, and Rachel had it with room to spare. She was the girl who, if you met her in the waiting room for an interview, you would walk out again.

No chance.

But Megan really liked Rachel. She was everything she wanted to be, but Dad had always prevented.

Ambitious. Clever. Determined. Beautiful.

The young woman never spoke about her family, but Megan assumed her folks backed her every step of the way. She'd come back home from college, and there would be dinner on the table, the walls stacked high with frames of diplomas, and certificates, and pictures of hockey teams, or netball, or fucking ballet.

If Rachel wasn't so quiet. So closed, maybe, Megan could have called her a genuine friend. But friends open up.

Instead she was - what was it? - a rival. A friendly rival, but a rival nevertheless?

It was all one way.

The Apprentice.

It was the bitches that always got furthest on that show. Some of them were dumb, that was obvious enough, but intelligence wasn't what got you hired.

Dad liked to watch *The Apprentice*. Megan hated it, but he always forced her to watch it instead of moping in her room.

It was all about the ability to play the game, make the right friends, make cold choices for your own greater good. Good fun to see those posh bastards get hammered, Dad would say. Never done a bit of work in their lives.

God, those *Apprentice* women were horrible, but look at them. The worst behaved and the best looking ones were those who'd got to stay week after week, along with the smarmiest of the boys.

But it was going to be a dog eat dog world out there in the City. If she was going to rise up the ranks, well, she would not get there by being all cupcakes, sweet smiles and letting the pretty girls and boys get on with it.

Dad didn't want her climbing any ladders. Not even to change gutters.

Rachel didn't seem to have the drive Megan did. She didn't *need* to escape her own father's underwhelming expectations. His warnings not to get ahead of herself. To be satisfied with her rightful place.

"So, what was this interview you're now more than...," Giles looked at his watch, "nearly two and a half full days late for."

"Oh, it was nothing," said Megan. "Hardly worth discussing now, is it?"

"No, sorry. I am interested. It came out wrong." Giles was trying to get the sarcasm out of his voice. Resolved from his time down the steps with Charles.

Sarcasm was the tone his workmates always used. Everything he'd learned at his secondary boarding school Winchester, and at Cambridge. He had to admit it: he was privileged. Never paid for anything in his life, never *really* paid. Mum and Dad took care of it.

He'd never strived, never had to work that hard. He'd detected Megan's panic about the job interview. He'd never had to sweat through a proper job interview. Never been turned down for a job. The CV did the work for him, and he'd even paid a career coach to write that for him.

Even his mental health problems had been taken care of, thanks to his parents' money.

He knew every word he said came out as a slight put down, even if it was good news or congratulations. Among his peers and their privilege, they never needed to take each other seriously. Never really had to sympathise.

It was the tone of voice he always heard in his head whenever those idiots from work or college were talking to him. Giving him a constant commentary about his every move. It was his own tone of voice. The one he was now coming to hate.

He felt bad for Megan. She was obviously struggling to gain success, and something else: was it pressure from her own upbringing? Essex girls don't make good, do they? They become hairdressers. Beauticians. Nail girls. They earn £8 an hour in tanning salons.

Giles took a deep breath and tried to make his voice as flat as possible. "Something in the City?"

"Just a legal secretary thing," said Megan, shying away. As if resigned to the fact that talking about anything was better than the endless silences echoing off the walls.

"It was a second interview, actually. I reckon I could have got this one too. I'd bought new clothes, done the whole thing."

"I'm sorry," he said. This time it didn't come out sarcastic.

"Thanks."

The two of them looked down at what they were wearing. Their once smart clothes were ragged and filthy with stains. Megan had blood on her toes. Her blouse was filthy.

The sleeves of Giles' Mark Powell shirt were soiled, and almost worn through at the elbow. Once pressed neatly and tucked into his trousers, it was now hanging out and grey.

It hung off him as if he'd lost pounds in the last few days. Actually, with nothing going in the right end and everything going out the other, there was every chance he had.

Despite their different backgrounds, Giles realised there wasn't much between all of them. Strip away the money, the privilege, the luck, and what was left?

With the hunger in their bellies and the thirst in their throat, all three of them were spending more and more time sleeping. Benny was resting right now, ten steps above.

The two smiled at their situation. "Well, I think you made a real effort. You look great."

She laughed and shook her head, a genuinely good humoured gesture.

Laughing Giles. This is new. Laughing is good, Giles. Next step, a little arm around the shoulder. Works every time, you know the drill.

Giles pushed the voices down.

"Go on," he said, trying again to keep the tone encouraging. "Please, I'm interested."

"Well, it was with Rank and Tudor. It's a little legal chambers close to Russell Square. That's where I was going before this," she lifted her palm limply. "It's not much but it's London, you know? The big smoke. Onwards and upwards?"

Onwards and upwards? Career girl. Say no more.

"Otherwise, it's just stay local in Epping. Living with Dad. Some crappy reception desk, in the same crappy town I grew up in. Serving people I went to school with."

Giles sighed.

"It's overrated, I promise you. The whole London thing. The suits, the fucking drinks after work."

The fucking of legal secretaries with tight asses after nights out in the pub after work.

He spoke more forcefully: "The dicks who you're forced

to work with. It's good for a time, sure, but just when you want to step off the escalator, take some downtime, appreciate - well, appreciate life - someone comes and puts another big escalator right there in front of you, and it's step on or get lost."

"All I want to do is get in on the first floor," said Megan. "Get a break. I can worry about the rest later?"

"Yeah, but later is when? Five years time? 10? 20? Time goes quick when you're supposedly having a good time, then boom. That was your life buddy, you happy now?"

Giles spat out the last words.

"Wow," said Megan. "That doesn't sound like the you I met a couple of days ago. I thought it was all '*A big firm, top for financial trading in Europe, actually.*'"

It was Giles' turn to shake his head and smile as Megan made fun of him. God, had he really said that? What a prick.

"Well, I guess there's nothing better for taking you off the escalator than forcing you to take the stairs."

Now they were really laughing. He'd made a genuinely funny joke.

Giles saw a gentle sparkle in Megan's eyes, even though the surrounding skin was grubby and the area around her eyes was puffy and raw from crying.

"You know, you're alright Megan."

"Giles." The retort was a matronly put down, an obvious rejection, but a friendly one.

Ah, just being coy, Giles. Show some balls.

"No, no, nothing funny. You're a genuinely great person."

She smiled shyly.

"And beautiful." He cringed at his own words. "I'm just saying, if I have to be stuck down an endless staircase, I'm glad it's with you."

This time Megan blushed.

This shit will work on anyone. That's your opening right there, Giles. Open permission if you ask me.

Fuck. He'd lost it. The calmness. The consideration. It was so hard to hold onto. The pill packet was empty. The pull of the voices too hard.

Giles shifted up one step towards Megan.

"Look, I know that you and Benny have got something going on, but given the circumstances, that doesn't prevent, does it, a little... It's just us down here, and we aren't going anywhere fast."

"Me and Benny do *not* have something going on. Christ, Giles, we're just trying to survive. What's your problem?"

"No problem," the sarcastic tone had returned. This was where it was sink or swim with the girls he chatted up. Drunk, of course.

The money shot Giles.

"I'm just trying to find a way into that beautiful head of yours."

The innuendo, so obvious to Giles and his voices, and blatantly obvious to Megan.

Will she bite?

"I'll tell you what Giles," said Megan snapping, and speaking loud enough to include the now awakening Benny into the conversation. "Since we're playing truths today, why don't you tell us all about your wife? You've kept awfully quiet, but we all want to know about her."

It was her turn to use a tone of voice loaded with sarcasm.

Giles' lips curled.

"That's right, isn't it Giles," she said, moving her own body two steps further towards the man above until she could feel his leg against her back. "We want to hear all about your wife. Lisa. That's her name, isn't it? If crying out in your sleep is anything to go by."

"Whoa," Benny said, dragging himself fully into consciousness. It took him a few seconds to read the situation as he sat up from his sleeping position.

"Giles? You're kidding right? You have a wife?"

26

G iles lit up. Four more left.

He had a wife. Past tense. Not that it was anyone else's business. Why did that lumbering hulk of meat always get in the way? What was he, Megan's guardian angel?

Muscling in. Guys like that may have all the brawn, but you can always teach them a lesson, Giles. Fucking oaf.

Giles moved his hand down and felt his wedding ring in his trouser pocket.

And she's too clever for her own good.

Someone had said it at work. When a man sees a woman for the first time, it's chest first then face. When a woman sees a man, it's wedding finger first. Then only assess the rest if it's all clear.

Megan must have seen Giles' wedding ring when they first came down the staircase, before he later slipped it off.

In the end, moving from sales into finance hadn't been too difficult for Giles. That Oxbridge degree, a few tweaked contacts - his friends actually earned commission if they introduced someone good to their firms - and Giles' natural sales charm got him a job on the finance floor of Herbert Ford Finance. From day one it would add 10k to his salary.

"Come on Giles, it's a straightforward decision. You should see some of the fringe benefits," his buddy David had said. Well, David wasn't really a buddy. He was a friend of an old college mate and he'd be making a bonus if Giles took the job. But circles could be tight in the City.

"It'll be long hours," Giles had told Lisa. "I'll probably have to be someone's underling for a while. At least until I get up there. It'll be more cash, private health care, gym membership for both of us. The lot."

"Will it make you happy?"

"It'll be a lot more pressure, but we'll be able to have the things we want."

"Then you should do it," said Lisa. "Hey, there's even this little Victorian terrace that's come up at Flixtons. With your new salary, we could make the mortgage. Just about."

Giles didn't use the gym membership in the first year. He didn't have the time. And the longer hours you worked, and the more hobnobbing with the partners after hours you did, the more you got on. Then you earned more, put in more hours, and became more senior. Then more hours, inside and outside of work. Then there were clients to take out.

"This is the big-time now, Giles," his manager Andrew Askew said over another pint after work after his first year and his third pay rise. "You could be Partner in a few years' time. Work hard now and you could retire in fifteen years. Lovely pad, lovely little wife at home, and nothing to do all day but drive in your Merc convertible to your second home in the countryside."

Giles and Lisa didn't move into that Victorian house. By

the time Giles was earning enough, it had long gone and other properties nearby had gone up and out of their reach. Instead, they'd bought a three bedroom terrace house further out in east London, close to Snaresbrook. Central Line to Central London. Perfect.

It was a little run down and Lisa was keen to get the main bedroom and the little box room redecorated, at least. But Giles said he didn't have the time to think about house repairs, let alone anything more major. He too often had to work late, and Lisa would spend evenings at home staring at the TV alone. It was that or the peeling wallpaper.

Got your pass stamped, Giles? Because the boys are off to The Fox to celebrate the latest round of bonuses. You in or out?

Giles was in. It was what was expected. It would be the second night this week of him rolling into Snaresbrook on the second-to-last train. Another night of fumbling his way noisily in the dark and landing into the bed next to Lisa stinking of booze.

He'd creep up to her, wanting to feel her warmth, but she'd shuffle away, letting cold air seep under the duvet between them. He'd creep closer and Lisa would shuffle again until she was almost balancing on the edge of the bed. Next morning he had no choice but to be out of the door early, grabbing a piece of toast to eat on his way to the Tube. He'd leave crumbs on the side and the knife sticking out of the margarine tub.

"I was thinking we could spend Sunday at my folks next weekend," said Lisa one Friday evening when Giles had come through the door by 8 p.m. He'd only stayed in the pub for a couple. "We've not seen them for ages. It's Mum's birthday."

"Ah, no-can-do," Giles replied. "There's this work thing. The boat race. We've got a corporate marquee at Mortlake.

You're invited, of course. But it'll be pretty intense. I assumed it wouldn't be your scene, really."

"How about the weekend after, then?"

"We'll have to see. I don't know if I'm coming or going right now at work. There's another promotion in the offing."

It's yours Giles, if you show willing. But you do need to show willing.

"But I never see you," said Lisa, "and... I thought we were building a life together here."

"Oh, by 'building a life together' you mean having a baby," said Giles. "This isn't about me at all, is it? It's about you." He spat the last words.

"No, it's not about me. I just miss *us,* Giles. It's not what I thought it would be like."

"What *did* you think it would be like? You told me to take the job. I'm doing this all for us, for our future."

"What, the drinking and the late nights and leaving me here by myself?"

"It's what we agreed. Work now, family later."

"We never said family later. We never even talked about family." Lisa had tears in her eyes. "What else did you think we were going to do? All my friends have babies or they're expecting."

"Yeah, and their husbands have all got decent jobs and can *afford* to have children."

"We can afford..."

"Maybe, but I'll never be here. I still need to put in the hours. I've got to earn the money to keep us: you, me, it."

"*It?*" Lisa really was crying now.

"You know what I mean. You'll be here with a baby while I go out and work."

"What, drinking with your mates?"

"It's not drinking with my mates, Lisa. It's the job. It's

what I do. It's my *job!* It's not some fluffy hobnobbing PR with celebrities you can choose to do or not." Giles was angry too now. He had to get out of here.

A few of us are getting together at The Fox, then onto a late bar. You in?

Giles hadn't changed out of his work clothes. "Fuck's sake," he said. He slammed the front door on his way out.

The next morning was Saturday. Despite a banging hangover, Giles had cooked Lisa scrambled eggs to eat in bed. Work was getting on top of him right now, he said. He was struggling to balance giving his all to the company and what he really wanted to do, which was spend time with her and build their own little nest.

That evening he surprised her with flowers and a restaurant booking at one of Liverpool Street's more upmarket eateries. The next day, they went to Lisa's parents' for an early birthday lunch. And Giles attempted to flatter her mum and praise her cooking. On the way home, he'd said they should take the weekend away soon. They could talk then more seriously about having a baby.

And Lisa agreed to go with Giles to watch the boat race.

Despite him being right about it not being her scene - too many suits talking about too much money - she'd admitted she enjoyed the race itself. She'd even cheered when the Cambridge crew crossed the finish line first and giggled with him about 'us trophy wives brought along for eye candy'.

His work colleagues weren't *that* bad either. Most were sober and, with their own girlfriends and wives about, obviously on their best behaviour. And to be fair, when she gave

Giles the glance that said *I've had enough,* he'd whisked her away.

They'd then gone for a private early evening meal at a quiet pub in Putney. That night they had better sex than Giles could remember. He'd been giving and tender; playfully resisting Lisa's usual demands to be tied to the bedposts until the last minute. Then he savoured the way, when he finally relented, that she shivered through waves of pleasure.

For another two or three weeks, he made it home earlier and only once or twice carried the stink of a pub back with him. But his absence from work didn't go without notice.

In *The Fox* one night, Asswipe had taken him aside. The other guys obviously already knew a *quiet word* was on the way. They'd scarpered outside with their pints, leaving the two of them alone at the end of the bar.

"Look, mate," said Andy. "We're all in this together. We've all got WAGS and they all get uppity every now and again. Buy them things and pay them a bit of attention, keep them sweet. You should bring her out here one night. It would be good to see her. But I do need you to get back on the team."

Giles felt like punching him. He'd never been pressured like this at his old job. And Lisa didn't need to be *kept sweet*. She was his wife, and he didn't want that lot leering over her if she came for a drink.

"This," Andy continued, swinging his glass around to encompass the pub. "This is what the job is *really* all about. You have to be able to relax. It's bonding time, it's why we work all together so well. Otherwise, how are you going to perform for me during the day?"

Perform. Giles stayed silent.

"See, you know I'm right. Listen, I've got good things

planned for you. Very good things. So let's have another pint, shall we? We can talk about those big things in the morning."

That night Giles missed the last Tube home. It was the first time he'd taken a late night taxi in a month.

But he got the impression Lisa was trying to be understanding too, to be more patient. She'd go out a little more often with her own friends, and say she didn't mind that he couldn't make Sunday dinner at her folks. Even when he had a free weekend and they went for a picnic or to see her friends, she only looked a little annoyed that Giles took calls on his mobile.

One Friday, Lisa had even suggested she pop into *The Fox* after a drink with her own friends. She said she wanted to get to know his work mates better, to see what all the fuss was about.

She was getting it now. Work now, life later.

Satpal and Simon and Tim remembered her from the boat race. They were welcoming, even charming. Giles saw her giggling in the corner as the boys sat around her, trying to outdo each other by cracking jokes. They bought her drinks, and no one said a word when she said she'd drunk enough booze and switched from white wine to lime and soda.

The boys kept on drinking, and Giles tried to keep up with them without showing Lisa how pissed he was getting. But at least she'd now understand what fun an after work drink could be; and how important it was for his career and their future for him to play the game.

It happened just before 11 p.m. when Giles was returning from the bar with a tray laden with another round: a few bottles for the lads, a soda and lime for Lisa and a pint - the last one he promised - for himself.

At first it looked like the boys were still cracking their jokes, sitting in the corner with Lisa in the middle. But as he approached, he could tell the atmosphere had changed. The boys were getting seriously close, and Lisa looked uncomfortable. When he reached them all, Lisa had already stood up. She gave him a wicked stare, and she had tears in her eyes. She pushed past Giles almost knocking the drinks tray out of his hands.

"Ooooh," the boys all laughed as she ran for the door.

Giles slammed the tray down and followed her out of the door. Her soda spilled all over the table, but the boys were too pissed to care. They just reached for their own bottles and chinked them together.

"Lisa, what's going on?" Giles said gently, a little too pissed. He grabbed her arm to prevent her from heading up the road. She swung around with a look of venom in her eyes. Yanked her arm out of his grasp. Giles thought she was going to throw a punch.

"Oh, you fucker," she said. There were no tears now, just pure anger.

"What, what?"

"You fucker. How dare you talk about our private life with your filthy mates?"

"What, what do you mean private life?" he put on a sympathetic voice, tried to hold her hand.

"Our fucking sex life, Giles," she threw his hand away.

"What? I didn't, I haven't. What are you talking about?"

"Yes, you have Giles, you bastard. They're probably in there laughing about it now."

"I don't know what you mean. I've never…"

She held up her finger to his face. "Don't you fucking lie to me Giles, just don't even try. I've just spent ten minutes being told by your mates about us having sex."

"Lisa, they're just fucking around. We're all pissed, you know..."

"No, Giles. I'm not pissed. And I've just been told by one of your greasy scum-bag pals he wishes his girlfriend would let him tie her up."

"Lisa..."

"God, Giles, one of them practically said he wanked over us doing it."

"They're just joking, Lisa. Anyone could have plucked that out of the air. Lots of people..."

"They didn't pluck it out of the fucking air Giles. They didn't pluck our wedding night out of the fucking air, did they? I can't imagine where they heard that from, Giles? You got any ideas?"

"Lisa, I love you," said Giles, reaching for her hand again. "I'm sorry. It's just talk. It's just what we do."

"Well, it's not what I do. This isn't me," she was crying now. A sickened cry of humiliation. "This isn't what I want. I can't do it anymore."

Lisa turned and headed quickly towards the Tube stop. Giles swore at himself as she walked away.

Yes, Giles *was* married.

But he hadn't seen Lisa for two months. There wasn't any paperwork yet, no legal letters, not even any deep and meaningfuls about how they might split the house they shared.

Lisa's dad phoned him a few days after she'd gone. He said she was feeling raw and could Giles step away for a little while? Let her get her head straight?

He hadn't, of course. He'd sent texts, most often in the

middle of the night. Texts after returning home with a belly full of booze to an empty home.

- Why don't you come back, we can talk?

- Thinking of you. Looking forward to holding you in my arms again.

- Miss you. I know you miss me. X

- You do miss me don't you? Call me. xxx

He'd duck outside of pubs in the City to get her on the phone, but it always rang a few times then went to answer phone.

"Lisa, hi love. I miss you. Call me back, eh? We can sort this out."

"Hey, it's me again. Just calling to find out how long you need. No pressure, I just miss you. Tell me what I can do."

"Hi, Lisa. I just want to hear your voice. Just as friends, okay? Please, call me back."

"Lisa, fucking hell - *guys, will you just shut the fuck up for a minute* - come on darling. Give me a call."

"Lisa, at least have the manners to return one of my calls. You are my wife, for God's sake. You owe me that."

Giles had parked outside her parents' house a couple of times. Okay, maybe three or four. There had been twitching curtains, but he didn't have the guts to go up and knock.

Lisa's dad Phil played flank occasionally, at one of the vets' squads at Basildon rugby club. His tone of voice on his third call to ask - 'I'm demanding this time' - that Giles give his daughter some space had carried a little more menace than Giles had cared for.

Eventually, Lisa's phone never rang at all. It just went to a dull tone. Line disconnected.

That's when Giles had stopped taking his prescription medication regularly. And started back on the recreational drugs with determination.

27

Megan lay on the dozen steps between Benny above and Giles below. She could hear the light breathing of Giles, his occasional twitching and light cries out as if harangued by terrible dreams. And who wouldn't have nightmares in a place like this?

It was a nightmare during the day, a nightmare during the night. Just living had become one terrifying ordeal. Everyone wants some separation from the world, even though we don't know what it's like. Now Megan knew, and she wanted more than anything else to get out of this isolation and darkness. And she never wanted to come back here again.

She heard Benny's deep breathing above her. She heard no restlessness or twitching. Megan couldn't put her finger on it. It was almost as if Benny hadn't been freaked out about this at all. The enforced darkness, the tough, cold, immovable walls. The silence, the nothingness. His reaction had been consistently calm and almost - what was it - welcoming? Familiar?

Whatever it was, it was the opposite of herself. Benny

was comfortable with his surroundings. Despite the hunger. Despite his injured foot. Despite the total blackness of night that continued to make Megan feel sick every time she gave it too much thought. Sick even though it had been a long time since she'd eaten anything to throw up. Her stomach growled.

But it wasn't her empty stomach or even being on the edge of total panic from the dark that was keeping Megan awake. It was her physical closeness to Giles. It was as if she couldn't escape him. She instinctively raised her bent legs a little further from the sound of his punctuated breathing below her.

The guy had acted like an idiot since they'd found themselves down here three days before.

But she'd seen his type before. Just trussed up peacocks really, full of themselves and their bonuses and their great jobs, but underneath - beneath those flashy feathers - there was little else. Lonely pointless lives. Take away the drink and the drugs, the matey bravado, and what were they really?

And this guy, down here, had revealed that loneliness behind the big talk, a deep sadness and vulnerability, when he had told them about Lisa.

The guy was hot and cold. One moment sweet and vulnerable. Almost charming, looking for affirmation. He could be funny. Megan remembered them laughing yesterday, but then look what had happened straight afterwards. Giles could become sarcastic and mean. Volatile, on the edge of being pushed too far. He was nasty and jittering. On the edge.

God, he'd been ready to snap since the moment they found themselves down here. Exactly the opposite of Benny.

Even the slightest provocation, and who knows what Giles could do.

Could he be dangerous? He certainly couldn't be trusted. Especially not in the dark.

Megan's eyelids were heavy and each part of her body, her aching bones and her painfully twisted, empty stomach, cried out for sleep. But confusion about Giles and fear of him kept her awake. Sitting up, she decided sleep would not come. She listened again to the two men breathing as they slept in the total darkness. Benny's regular rhythm was like a soothing seashore.

It was a risk, but could she?

Megan edged up a few steps, trying to move her body as quietly as possible. She felt her arm brush against the man's legs above, and then his belt. Silently, her body came to rest against Benny's ribs. He was still sleeping. She felt the slow rise and fall of his side against her body, a warm and welcoming feeling making Megan feel safer.

Gently, ever so slowly, Megan brought her head to rest on Benny's chest, trying not to wake him. Listening for a change in his breathing as her ear pressed closer to his body. As she lay her head down, she felt the rough arm which Benny had drawn across his chest. A self-comforting sleeping position.

As she enjoyed the warmth of Benny's arm muscles as they pressed against her cheek, she detected a change in the man's breathing. It stopped for a moment. Megan felt Benny's arm lift, pushing her face away from him, her head suddenly disconnected from his body. She had got it wrong. Was he pushing her away?

But she felt the arm move across her face and wrap gently around the back of her neck. There was no force to it, but the arm exerted a gentle pull that encouraged Megan to lay her head fully onto Benny's chest. Then it pulled her whole body closer. She wrapped herself into the side of the man as she lay her own arm across his stomach, moulding into his torso.

Most of her remained pressed up against the cold concrete of the steps beneath them both, but where their bodies connected, she felt a comfort, warmth and closeness.

She listened as Benny's breathing slowly became deep again. She allowed the weight of her own eyelids to exert their pressure, trying to forget Giles and the dark and the suffocation of the situation which she knew would still be there when she woke up again.

Within minutes she fell into a deep calm, her breathing matching the deep inhalation of the man in whose arms she had finally allowed herself to fall asleep.

28

Megan was on her class WhatsApp group. She hadn't added herself to it, but one way or another her number had been added and her phone started ping-ping-pinging with notifications.

She looked at the general gist of the conversation. Rarely were the girls asking for help with the college work. More like organising nights out; sizing up the likelihood that the barista in Starbucks was gay, and if not, which of the girls might get him into bed first; sharing inspirational quotes and inappropriate memes.

Megan didn't join in the chatter, except to respond if someone needed a copy of a sheet they'd not picked up from class. Or needed help to understand what a 'growth curve' was. She was always thanked with smiley faces, pumping hearts, and thumbs up.

She'd rather have not been on the group at all, but she knew that 'Megan has left this chat' always said more than, 'I just don't want my phone pinging all day'.

She turned off notifications, so the WhatsApp chat just built on her phone into tens, twenties and thirties of messages a day in silence. She rarely looked at it. Nobody seemed to notice that she rarely joined in.

But Megan had to check her other WhatsApp messages frequently, because Dad was always monitoring her.

Woe betide her if she ignored a message from him, even for an hour or two. She'd tried to convince him to use SMS messaging, but he said WhatsApp was free and all of his clients were on it. She shouldn't get special treatment.

It was a Friday night. Some girls were obviously out drinking, either together or in separate groups, or even at home with booze and a movie.

Normally she'd scroll past the NVQ Chat group without glancing at it. But like the cocktail effect, when you hear your name said in a crowded room, she couldn't help her eye catching the word 'Megan' with a laugh/crying emoji next to it.

Instinctively, she opened up the chat.

The girls were idly bantering about which of the pupils was most likely to succeed in life. A few names had gone around the chat, with the girls poking fun at each other.

'Jodie, most likely to succeed working in a tanning salon!' With grinning, brown faced girl emojis.

Jodie had then posted.

'Taylor: definitely Botox and fake boob clinic.'

'Hey, I'm proud of these puppies.' Then some dog face emojis. 'Nominate Sharon for barmaid.'

'Hic!' Sharon had replied. 'You won't get me on that side of the bar. Ever! Make mine a double, while you're at it!! Who's buying.'

Laugh emoji.

Cry emoji.

Pint glass emoji.

And so the chat went on. Banter, making fun, wasting time. Drunk chat.

And then it happened.

'Most likely to come top of the class?' It was a post from Taylor.

'Megan!' That was Jodie again.

Megan was embarrassed. She saw the cursor blinking, begging for her to answer before someone else did.

She typed: 'Surely that's Rachel. She's put in SO much work.' Then added a wink emoji.

It was time Rachel got recognised, she thought. She pressed send without hesitation.

Only someone else's message had popped up before hers.

'Who's most likely to succeed sleeping their way to the top?'

Her own message appeared directly afterwards.

"Fuck," shouted Megan, as she realised how the WhatsApp thread now read.

"No, no!"

She threw her mobile onto her bed in horror, swung around, grasping her face with both hands. What had she done?

She went back to her phone. The chat had erupted with laughing, winking, and angel emojis.

Seemed like everyone had something to say.

'It's the quiet ones you have to watch.'

'Wondered why she's always first into class and last out!'

'Innocent Lady Suck Suck, here's your Grade A'

It was funny, because Rachel was so incredibly unlikely to be what Megan had just suggested. They were making the most of it.

But as all social media chats do, it wound and warped and swept like a crowd of starlings over a bridge.

Suddenly girls were calling Rachel 'privileged', 'posh', 'full of herself', 'can't be bothered with us', 'too good for us all'

Drunk talk. A few moments of silence on the chat group before talk moved on to something new.

Then there was a single message.

'Rachel has left this group'

The chat went into uproar again.

'Ooops!'

'Can't take a joke.'

'See what I mean?'

'Fucking snob.'

And on it went. The discussion of the night. The victim of the night.

Only Megan knew how much those messages would have hurt Rachel. She received harsh enough ones from her Dad. She hadn't even known Rachel was on the chat.

She panicked.

Should she leave the group? All that would do would put her in the firing line.

Should she post in Rachel's defence? Explain herself? In their drunken state, the girls wouldn't care. They wouldn't have even remembered how the conversation started.

She took a deep breath and called Rachel.

Call rejected.

She called again.

Call rejected.

Frantically, Megan texted: "Rachel, so sorry. I can explain. Please pick up the phone."

Call rejected.

Megan's heart began beating fast. She could feel the

beginnings of a panic attack. She *needed* to get through to Rachel.

Call rejected.

She screamed out. "Please!"

She tried one more time.

'The number you are calling is not available at this time.'

No message facility.

Megan started stamping her feet. Banging the walls.

Her bedroom door opened.

"What the hell is going on, Megan?" her dad shouted. "I'm trying to watch *The Apprentice.*"

Over the next few weeks, Rachel started missing classes. No one spoke to her.

Megan caught her a few times in the corridor, tried to say sorry, that she wanted to explain. Rachel said it was okay. She knew social media was a minefield.

"Coffee?"

"No, I'm busy right now. Got a lot going on. See you around." Then she'd be gone.

She didn't answer Megan's calls or respond to her texts.

"Ah, Miss Prim and Proper isn't bothering anymore," one tracksuit said.

"Fucking snob thinks she doesn't need to come to class," said Taylor.

When Rachel did come in, Megan watched her as she manoeuvred her way through groups of girls standing in the corridor. The conversation would go quiet as she passed. Some of the girls would fold their arms over their fake boobs, creating an even thinner corridor for her to pass through.

"Is everything okay, love?" Megan asked her in the library. "Not seen you around too much. I saved some notes for you."

"Thanks, Megan," Rachel said, her cheeks going slightly pink.

Megan said she regretted the confusion.

"Hey you want to come over to mine? I want to explain everything. Make up for it. I really didn't mean for *that* to happen. We'll have a Chinese meal or something?"

"Sure,' said Rachel. "That'll be nice."

It was a start.

But Megan never got a chance to follow through.

Megan was there when it happened. She wished she hadn't been. She wished to goodness she hadn't been on that WhatsApp group. That she had been brave enough to get out, right from the start. She wished she could turn back time.

She was guilty. By doing nothing. By not fighting back that night, when the girls were making their barbed comments.

By not explaining the mistake she'd made to them. By not defending Rachel. She was guilty as hell.

The entrance to the main college building was all broken paving slabs. Rachel was coming in behind Taylor, heading for one of the last classes before the term ended.

Legs got tangled, and Rachel pitched over and off a step. It was all a bit of a mishmash, and she went down hard. Rachel hit her cheek on the concrete.

There was not much blood, nothing broken. She sat up, dabbing at a graze across her left cheek with a tissue. A few students crouched down to make sure she was okay. Plucking her from the floor.

"Oh, my God Rachel, are you okay?" Megan said,

running up to where she had fallen. "Oh darling, what happened?"

"It was nothing," Rachel had said. "Just a trip."

As she sat there on the concrete, Rachel's beautiful green eyes were red and damp. Full of grief. Asking: Why?

Rachel never turned up to class that day. She didn't turn up the next day either. Nor the next week. Then it was end of term.

Megan tried to get hold of her by phone. She'd sent texts, made calls.

Rachel never replied.

29

There was something Giles knew that Megan and Benny didn't. When he awoke and saw Megan and Benny lying together on the steps above him, he saw no point in keeping it quiet any longer.

He might even get Benny back on side.

Just another puff, Giles? Just another pint? A shot before home time? Just another line? You know you can never say no to a little uplift, Giles. All the lads are having one.

Giles was so despairing down in that hole that nothing mattered any more.

What difference would it make if he did the coke he had in a little plastic bag in the pocket of his suit jacket? There wasn't a lot there. Just a few lines' worth, the remnants of *that* night.

Giles sniffed. That had been mental. He and his work-mates had been taking themselves off to the toilet all night, sitting on the pan and snorting little white lines from the backs of their hands. By the time Giles fell out of the Casino, he was too far gone to take any more.

There was something else he wanted, something he

knew he could get not too far from the City. The coke had gone back into the corner of his pocket: a little something to spice up tomorrow night, or whenever else his workmates insisted it was time to go out on the town again.

Supping, snorting and sucking tonight, Giles? You know it makes sense.

But down here? Well, there was no tomorrow. The walls were oppressive, the unending light feeling like he was under interrogation, being forced to confess. Giles needed to relax, to take his mind off being trapped. He reached down into his pocket, pulled out the little bag, and waved it at Megan.

"Hey, you want some of this?"

Megan woke, rubbed her eyes and pulled herself from Benny a little. Giles asked again.

She shook her head. And not just to say 'no', Giles felt. It was as if she was sorry for him. He baulked at her judgement. Naive little Essex girl, living with Daddy somewhere at the end of the Central Line. What did she know about stressful life in the City.

Keep climbing that ladder, sweetheart. Sleep with those you need to and you'll get there. Then you can play with us big boys. Big boys like me.

Giles shook his head.

Megan might be patronising, but those guys from work were worse. For them, you could never snort *enough* coke, never drink *enough* pints, or shots, or whatever it was they'd decided the tipple was tonight.

I'd like to see you guys down here. You'd be shitting your pants. Hell, he was shitting his pants. Or at least he had given up.

Nothing mattered: not the booze, the girls, the credit

cards, the bonuses, and definitely not the drugs. None of it had never had mattered. Except for Lisa.

This isn't for the kicks. Giles stared down at the little pouch. This is to numb the pain, smooth the edges of these stairs, interrupt the endless starkness of this light.

Back up there, he *wanted* the coke along with the pints.

But down here? Down here, he *needed* it.

"Benny?" The guy had woken too now, and looked over as Giles waved the pouch towards him. "A little something to pass the time?"

Come on you pussy. It's no fun alone. What's a little coke between friends?

Benny stared at the package and then Giles with sorrowful eyes. He took a deep breath and slowly whistled it out, shaking his head. But Giles could see a longing in his face.

"Not me, man," said Benny. "It ain't me. Not any more."

Benny had learned a lot on the Programme. About clarity and understanding his position. Stevie had talked about not letting things get out of control. But most important was Benny coming to understand his weaknesses and triggers. Even the slightest waver could knock him off his feet again. Everything Benny had worked for, all the difficult decisions he'd been forced to make.

They'd all be for nothing, and he'd be back to the start.

Going cold turkey in prison was horrible. Benny needed drugs like he needed air. The methadone the Programme had put him on hadn't eased the craving, but the prison walls that kept him in gave Benny no choice but to take what they would give him.

But day followed day. Benny felt the pain ease and then - on the surface at least - go away. He came to hate that he'd become dependent, that the heroin and crack had left him out of control, that he could tip back into it any time. But coming to understand he was a drug addict was the easy part. Prison was the easy part.

What he had to do afterwards, that was where the real pain was. There could be no compromise. He may be off drugs, but he would always be an addict. Staying out of the way of temptation meant Benny had to leave everything he'd ever known. Get away from his old life. Never even consider going back to where he used to live.

Rachel had come to see him in prison.

In here, Benny was safely tucked away from that old life. Rachel, his love for her, was the only gateway back to the old world. If he allowed that door to remain open, the temptation to walk through would be too strong.

He decided not to go down to see her when she came. Maybe in a month or two, when he was stronger. Next time she came, he promised, he'd go down.

Rachel didn't come back. She was probably too out of it to haul herself out of bed. Benny knew what that was like. Someone else was scoring for her now, feeding her habit. Providing a bed for her.

Rachel had walked into Benny's life with £50 and a plea for oblivion. It was £50 he was happy to take, and the oblivion he delivered in the form of crack cocaine.

He didn't consider himself a drug dealer. He'd just bought more than he needed and started selling it to friends, maybe their friends, for a bit of profit so he could go and buy more. He'd get his own hit, they'd get theirs and there'd be more for tomorrow. A proper little entrepreneur.

Benny's council flat, four storeys up on the Cracknel

Estate close to Bethnal Green was always full of people. They were quiet there, not raucous. No late night parties or violent scrabbles with the cops. People came, handed over the money, maybe smoked a little something, slumped on the sofa or a mattress on the floor, then went away again.

A few of Benny's bigger mates had appointed themselves the 'heavies' and Benny was happy to slip them £20 every now and again or stand them a hit just for being around. They had to have a quiet word with a few flat visitors, once or twice frisked people they didn't know - weapons or police wires, they'd imagined they were looking for - but had never raised a hand to anyone. Being there was enough to emphasise that this was a quiet operation. A few mates hanging out on the quiet. Definitely *not* a crack den.

The girl appeared out of nowhere, brought in by some Kurdish lads Benny vaguely knew from around the Turkish bars on the Dalston Kingsland Road. Benny had chatted to Rachel for a while, just to check her out - to make sure she wasn't a cop, or worse a plant from one of the east London drugs cartels doing a recce on the flat.

She had limp hair and was so gaunt her collar bones showed through her light top. But she had a natural beauty about her, the hint of a sparkle in her deep green eyes. But she didn't smile once. This one had potential, thought Benny. Not just for a sale, but maybe something else. He gave the Kurds some money to go away.

It wasn't usual for Benny to share a hit with someone who came to buy. He preferred to do it among very close friends once the evening's trade had dried up. She'd done some heavy drugs before. That was clear from the paleness of her skin and the bruises on her arms, but she seemed to be seeking more than just a single hit. She seemed lost and unsure, even naïve.

The crack they shared on a mattress on the floor in a room at the back brought a huge grin to Benny's face and a smile cracked on the girl's thin lips too. They'd chatted quietly for a while about not much, then both lain back and fallen asleep next to each other.

When he woke an hour later, her eyes were already open, and she was blinking at the ceiling. But she didn't move from out of his arms or move her head away from his. They lay there as it got dark, until eventually she sat up, put her hand gently on Benny's chest and told him she had to go.

Benny gave her a small wrap of cocaine to take with her, and when she said she didn't have any money, he told her to pay him next time. Now she offered him a genuine smile, much more beautiful and relaxed than the grin the drugs had brought out an hour before.

"Do you have to go," he asked, clasping his hand over hers. For a moment he saw a desperation in her eyes, as if she was going to lie back down, allow Benny to hold her in his arms and just sleep. But just as quickly her face went steely and her eyes took on a blank look. She pulled her hand away and stood abruptly, making for the door.

A boyfriend, was that it? Benny felt a bit offended by the sudden change in atmosphere. He felt jealous. Another hit when she'd gone would take care of that. Anyway, the £50 and the last hour more than made up for any annoyance he felt now.

"Let me give you my number," he said, scribbling it on the back of an unopened piece of junk mail. "For next time, so you don't have to come through those Dalston boys."

She dropped her coldness and smiled again as she took it. Someone showed her to the front door, as Benny sat in the bedroom with others popping their head round the door offering knowing jokey eyes.

"Ah, fuck off, will you?" he told them. He knew they'd assume she exchanged sex for drugs, and he wasn't about to put them right. He certainly would not tell them that all they'd done is share a hit and then lain there together in the quiet. That for once in his life, and just for ten or twenty minutes, Benny had felt he could be truly happy.

A few hours later he received a text message from a number he didn't know.

- Thank you for this afternoon... whatever it was. Sorry I had to leave. I had to work. Will have more money to spend soon and I'd like to spend it with you.

Rachel was a mix of hot and cold as they got to know each other over the following months. And eventually they started sleeping together. Sometimes she was open and talkative and would drop her guard to reveal smiles and even a laugh. But often she was cold and formal: just wanted the drugs, to hand over the money and get out of there.

Benny learned by implication that Rachel was selling sex, though she never actually said it. He didn't want her to say it out loud, as if it would sully her. But he knew he didn't want her to do it, either.

He started giving her hits, then when she rose to leave and tried to hand over money he'd refuse and she'd curl back into bed and they'd fall asleep together for the entire night. She talked little about herself, always clammed up if Benny asked too much. But it was clear she was lonely, had nothing else to fill her time, and Benny hoped she enjoyed his company.

Life was complicated. It wasn't a relationship, as such. It was mixed up with the drugs and the money and a chaotic fug of addiction.

One directionless day followed another. Hit followed hit. Benny would go out with his friends on jobs; thieving, a little light mugging, just enough to feed their habits and feed themselves. Benny and Rachel would lie in bed afterwards, next to filled ashtrays and empty cans, enveloping each other, looking at the ceiling waiting for slow warm creep of the craving to kick in again.

Slowly, she stopped disappearing in the evening. Then not at all. She smiled more. Laughed. She declared she would only sleep with him from now on. Maybe even get a proper job.

In prison, he'd tried to tell them about Rachel. There was someone they should help. But it was one of those things Stevie was always saying.

"It's crazy, really Benny. We're only funded to help former offenders, not those who might offend. Those who are already at risk."

'At risk' was the Programme's word for everyone like Benny. Criminals. Druggies. Prostitutes. Stevie had swung his lanyard and shaken his head at the twisted logic of it. Benny knew he had to let her go if he was to stay clean.

Rachel not coming back to visit him in prison was probably the best thing for him. Though it hurt far worse than any cold turkey.

Benny sat on his cold step. He couldn't really have loved Rachel. If he did he wouldn't have left her like that in East London. He wouldn't have saved himself by never going back there.

Yeah, prison was easy.

30

The worst thing about it, thought Benny, was not that he had relented. It was how easily he had given up.

Giles had not had to beg. Giles hadn't had to pester him, wheedling out months of Programme messaging.

From the moment he'd seen the bag of coke, Benny knew he would take it. It made him sick how weak he was. He couldn't even blame his need to escape from the relentless pain in his injured foot. His foot had gone practically numb, as if there was no life left in his lower right leg at all.

And it was as simple as that. That old need suddenly started running through his veins; the adrenaline pumped into his brain and he felt his breath quickening. A warm feeling rose into every inch of his skin. He imagined the satisfaction, the immediate release. Release from this spiral, from the memories, from his life that was going nowhere. Just something different from trying to keep it together.

Benny poured out a small pile of the powder onto his palm and passed the pouch back to Giles. He looked at Megan, but she wouldn't meet his eye. Giles sprinkled out a thin strip on the back of his hand and ran his nose across it.

Benny dabbed the pool, held a coated finger to his nostril, and sniffed deeply. He put the finger down and took up another finger's worth, holding it to the opposite nostril. He held up his palm and sniffed in the remains deeply. A few grains were left. He licked his finger and dabbed them around his palm, then rubbed the remaining coke into his gums. For a moment Benny felt the deepest sorrow, a painful grief. He had a feeling towards Giles that bordered on hate.

And then, despite himself, he loved him.

"Oh yeah," said Giles, as Megan watched him snort the final bits of coke from the back of his hand.

"Yeah," he said again, as he stuck out his tongue, directing a disgusting licking gesture towards her.

"You don't know what you're missing, baby," he said. He stuck his tongue into the tiny plastic bag to mop up the remaining minuscule grains. Then he spat the plastic off his tongue in Megan's direction.

"You're a disgusting pig," she said, looking at Benny for reassurance. But the bigger man just sat there with his head pulled back, eyes tightly closed, deeply breathing with a slim smile on his face.

"Benny?" she asked. He barely waved a hand, as if dismissing her.

Little girl.

The smile on Giles' face widened into a wicked grin.

"You and me," he whispered, his eyes narrowing and staring directly at her chest. He pulled his hand towards his crotch, fondling for a second. "You and me," he repeated, then nodded towards Benny, "and him too."

"You're both filthy pigs," Megan spat, standing up. As she stomped between them, she felt her blood pumping heavily in every vein as adrenaline and fear rushed around her body. She quickened her step, moving upward and away from the pair.

She could feel blood pulsating in her temples, her face flushing crimson, as she climbed two, sometimes three steps at a time.

I have to get out of this hole. Giles is a fucking animal. But Benny? From the start of this... this, whatever this *thing* was, she'd trusted him.

God, she *needed* him.

Benny had been the only barrier between her and... She tried to put the thought out of her mind, but there was nowhere for it to go. Her anger had stripped away any hiding place for even the most horrifying of thoughts.

Benny was the only barrier between her and Giles. The guy was unhinged.

Without Benny, she realised as she continued upward, she was completely alone.

"You fucking bastard, Benny," Megan shouted down, feeling bile rising in her mouth and spitting it down the way she had come. She wiped the drops of spittle away from her mouth.

"Fucking men," she shouted. "Every one of you. Fuck you. Fuck you. Fuck you." She was shouting aloud what she often said in her dreams.

To her Dad.

She looked above her, but saw only more steps. Steps, steps, steps. She was going to get attacked by these guys and there'll be no one to even hear her scream. No one to help. No way to fight them off.

"No," she screamed. "No. Oh, Jesus, no."

The anger was unbearable, and she felt the panic. The deep black panic of the black bin, the same blind panic of when the lights first went off. It hit her in crashing wave after wave. She hammered on the tiles above the bannister. She rushed with pleasure as shooting pains shot up her arms and as her palms connected with the cold ceramic.

She turned around, rage and hysteria having fully taken hold, and steadied herself against the bannister. She kicked out at the centre of the spiral, first with one bare foot and then another.

"You fucking, fucking bastards," she screamed. "I have to get out of here."

"I," she kicked, "have", kick again, "to", kick, "get out". She watched with satisfaction as blood leaked through her grubby tights. Better. Pain and release in equal measure.

She span around on her bloodied, thinly covered feet and grabbed the iron rail with both hands. She let out a scream and yanked on the rail with all of her strength. Nothing moved. She yanked again, then again, screeching obscenities at the top of her voice with every pull. She could see her fingers turning white at the pressure and felt deep grooves forming in her palms where they pulled and pushed the metal.

Yank. Yank. Again, it felt good. She felt control. A focus for her rushing pulse.

"You fucking bastard." She was addressing the rail, then the tiles, then the steps, the dark, the spiral, the world. Her own father. She stopped and looked at her hands. They were white with deep red lines across them.

"Oh, please someone help me." Her words were slower now. The words mumbled through tears that welled up, enveloping the anger and helping it to dissipate. Her panic ebbed away, to be replaced by only vacant despair.

"Oh God," she cried, turning and sitting down onto a step, not caring about the pain as her backside hit the tough concrete. "Shit. Shit. Shit."

Megan drew her legs up to her chest, tucking her bloodied feet towards her as tightly as she could. She plunged her head between her legs and threw her arms over her neck, grasping them together over her shoulders, pulling her whole body deeper in. As she sobbed, she tried to pull herself into such a tight ball that it might crush itself. Draw into itself so tightly, so small that it would simply disappear. Rubbed out like a disappearing star. Leaving this. Leaving it all behind.

Megan sat in her tight ball, the tears now streaming freely from her tightly closed eyes and dripping onto the concrete below. She could feel her heartbeat slow and she rocked on the step in time with its beats, trying to gather some comfort from the rhythm, trying to find that baby-like calm an infant sometimes finds when held close and rocked by a parent.

Megan's panic attack calmed. All that was left were deep tears of loss and grief.

Megan didn't remember that ever happening. Being rocked by a parent. Or even hugged.

Rachel's parents would have hugged her. Consoled her about the WhatsApp bullying. They may even have encouraged her to be in touch with Megan again.

Or maybe Rachel's dear parents suspected what Megan herself thought. She envied Rachel. Pictured her as girl perfect. A warm and giving home life. Freedom. Good looks and intelligence. She had everything that Megan didn't.

Even now, Megan wasn't sure. She wasn't clear. She

wasn't *absolutely* certain that she hadn't sent that WhatsApp message on purpose.

She thought of Dad and *The Apprentice*. Was she really a sneaky, treacherous, bad ass bitch like the women on that show?

The one who ended up on top, whatever the cost?

31

Giles watched Megan come down the stairs and rejoin the group. She sat above Benny, keeping her legs curved and sideways, as if she was shielding herself from them both.

You're a shit, Giles. You're a waste of space.

Benny was dozing again, the coke having satisfied something in him, allowing him to pass out.

Giles was rocking slightly on his step. Like he was shivering slightly.

"Sorry, sorry, Megan, like sorry. Didn't mean to upset you, Megan. Sorry."

You fucking worthless piece of shit.

"Are you okay Giles," Megan said, looking down at the floor, clearly avoiding looking him in the eye.

"Yes, yes... just, I guess, just the comedown. Always makes me a bit. I don't know, shaky."

Giles nibbled on his nails. Scratched his teeth against his lips.

Worthless. Wannabe. Lightweight. Rapist.

"I'm not," Giles shouted.

"What, you're not okay?"

"Not, not, not." His eyes were twitching. His neck was ticcing.

Filthy fucking whore. Good-for-nothing husband.

"Giles," said Megan more loudly, trying to smooth out her fear into a soothing tone.

"'Sokay, 'sokay," he said. "My drugs. I've missed them."

Benny woke and sat up. Giles watched the two chatting.

"Benny, he's gone weird."

"Hey, man, you alright down there?"

"Yes, yes. Just medicine. Run out."

Needy, crazy bastard.

"Run out of coke?" said Benny.

Giles shivered. And ticced.

"Wait," Megan whispered to Benny.

She spoke gently: "Giles, do you take medicine? A prescription."

Giles nodded, wrapping his arms around himself.

"'Sokay, need to sleep, need to calm down."

Disabled twat. Can't do without his pills.

"Is it epilepsy, Giles? Or ticcing? Tourettes? Are you missing your medication?"

Giles rocked back and forward. He nodded.

"Bi-polar," he said.

Say it, say it, you pansy. Tell them we're here. Let us out, you freaking mental case.

"Voices," he said. "Mental. Mental."

"It's okay," Benny said to Megan. "I've seen this before. Cold turkey. He's on some kind of medication, and he's run out down here. I should have seen it a mile away. The coke has turned his mind to mush without his meds."

"Giles, can you hear me?" said Benny.

"Yep, yep."

Big man. Boss man.

"Great, listen mate, we're going to look after you, right? Do you have any more medication with you?"

Giles shook his head.

"Okay, you need to sleep, okay? Relax. Do you have any cigarettes left?"

Giles pulled one out. His hands shook. He flicked his lighter several times. His hands too shaky to get it lit. Finally, he got a flame, touched the tip and drew deeply on the cigarette.

"That's it, mate, enjoy the fag. Concentrate on the cigarette."

His hands stopped shaking as he drew the smoke into his lungs, and the nicotine flowed through his bloodstream.

They all sat in silence while he finished it.

"That's it now, Giles. Sleep for a while, eh? Have a decent sleep."

Giles put his head against his arm and lowered himself down onto the step.

Ah, spoil sport. We'll be back, though. You know we will. We all need to get out of this place. And you know, don't you Giles, you know there's only one way to free them?

"How's your foot?"

"Stiff, but not so painful now."

"Would you like me to?"

Megan asked, only after looking towards Giles who was now passed out on the steps with nearly a full twist below them.

"That would be good, Megan."

She moved down from her position above the man until

she reached foot level. Like she had the day before, she gently lifted his foot into her lap. He lifted his thigh to help.

Benny winced, but relaxed again once his heel was planted firmly on her upper knees.

She didn't know what she was doing. She'd never had a professional massage in her life, and certainly didn't need one. That's all posh girl stuff, her Dad would say, nothing better than getting out there for a walk or doing a hard day's graft.

Megan took Benny's calf muscle and squeezed it gently, finding sinews and attempting to run stiff fingers down them.

Benny groaned a little, a mix between pain and satisfaction. Perhaps some pleasure.

"How's that feel Benny?"

"It feels good, thank you."

She continued, inventing the squeezes and pushes and pressure points as she went along.

Apart from occasional winces, Benny hummed and nodded his head in all the right places.

"Can I ask you something, Benny? If it's not too personal?"

"Not sure we can get much more personal," the man said.

"It's just that, well, you seem so at ease down here. You've seen me and Giles. Charles too. It's been wild for us. But you've been, well, so comfortable."

Benny took a deep breath. It seemed to Megan she'd pushed too far. And then Benny spoke.

"Two months ago I was living in prison."

Megan nodded. She was cross with herself for the assumption. But she'd been right.

"Don't worry. I didn't do anything too crazy. Fist fights.

Some dealing. The thing they got me on was armed robbery. A petrol station. The guns weren't even loaded."

"I'm sorry Benny," said Megan.

"Jeez, nothing to be sorry for. No one got hurt but us assholes. I deserved the six years they put me away for. Did four years, then got out because I agreed to get on a transition programme."

"I understand," she said.

"Those first few weeks, Megan? You think you're special. Like you've been rewarded or something for being a criminal. Then the walls start to get you down. You realise you can't walk out of that place. You bang on the walls. You bang on the doors. You plead with the guards. You're sick to the stomach with withdrawal.

"But you know, as you lie there in your bunk each night, however hard you bang on those walls, they aren't going away. At least not until someone on the outside decides it's time to let you out.

"Some of the guys, you know, they can't take it. Comes out as aggression. Fighting. Attacking the guards. Setting light to their cells.

"Others. Well, they can't take it in different ways. God help them. There's always a way to kill yourself in prison."

"And the rest," asked Megan. "You?"

He shook his head.

"Acceptance, maybe? They offered me the Programme. To deal with my drug addiction. To help turn my life around. It starts in prison, then you get out into the community for a while. But it's tough. Like, so tough not to go back to your old life."

"Hence the walls?"

"Yeah, I'm kind of comfortable down here. I feel safe, from myself. I was desperate to go back to where I started out. Get back into drugs. Find my girl, again. Maybe this," Benny indicated the spiral staircase, "maybe this is my warning. I don't believe in any kind of God, Megan, but if this is life teaching me a lesson, then it's one I needed to learn."

"You said, girl?" she said, momentarily stopping the massage.

"Long gone. I let her down. Had to let her down, for my own sake. To stay on the Programme."

"That's so cruel."

"Megan, I'm lucky. I got clean. And when I took that coke today, it reminded me how lucky I've been. Because if I'd have been up there, I'd have gone straight back to the old neighbourhood for another hit. Down here, no more hits. No choice. Just a reminder that it isn't where I want to be. Like I say, I'm lucky. Girl or no girl."

"Some kind of luck," said Megan. She moved up and sat next to Benny. She put her arm around him.

"I think you've been very strong. I can't imagine how hard it's been. We're all only in so much control of our lives, but seems to me you've steered yours towards a good place. You should be admired for that."

"I don't know, Megan," he said. "I've done bad things."

"And it's time to forgive yourself," said Megan. "That's the last hurdle, and you need to get over it."

Together, they looked down at the spiral below, Giles still sleeping.

Megan whispered.

"You said you'd seen it before?" She nodded towards Giles.

"Been through it," Benny said. "Pretty much every other inmate, too. Cold turkey. They bring you in, and every one of us is surviving on drugs of one form or another. Me, it was coke and heroine. They try to replace it, but you'd tear the

GIDEON BURROWS

place down for another real hit. You kick, you scream, the voices in your head taunt you.

"You end up a shivering wreck on the floor, then slowly the doctors, the guards, they pick you up again. You learn to live without the drugs.

"But some guys, they got mental health, you know? I saw it from the start here. I reckon you did too. That guy's shaky. Super friendly one time, then out of his mind another. Crude even. Jokey, then filthy talk."

"I've seen him ticcing, mumbling to himself," said Megan.

"He said he was bi-polar, and on medication. The coke was a trigger for some kind of episode. All respect to him, but Giles is a head case."

Benny continued: "You heard him talk about his medication, that he'd run out? Seems to me he's been on those drugs long term, to keep him straight. Down here, he doesn't have the medication. Whatever mental health problem he has, it's going to get worse."

"What do you mean," whispered Megan.

"He's not safe down here," said Benny. "He's a threat to himself mainly, but to us, too. I've seen schizophrenics without their medication, they'll tear you apart. They imagine you're the devil, or a dragon, or a witch. Or whatever the hell the voices say. And they'll do whatever the voices in their head tell them to do."

The two sat silently, watching Giles as he took deep breaths in his sleep.

"Will you protect me, Benny, if it came to it?" said Megan.

"We're going to have to look after each other. Giles is going to be totally unpredictable when he wakes up. I've an idea, but it's all in or out. "

"I'm in," said Megan. "I trust you Benny. I don't know if we're going to get out of this staircase alive, but we need some control over whatever future we have left."

Benny put his arm around her and pulled Megan in tight.

32

By the time Giles left the casino he was no longer rolling drunk, just dizzy and already on his way to a hangover. The guys had dropped away over the last hour, some with girls they'd met. But most just disappearing to stagger down the casino steps and into a cab.

Giles hadn't meant to be last out of the door, but suddenly he could no longer recognise any of the punters around the gaming tables. And there were no girls left at all in the club. He'd been gamely trying to chat to the few women in the casino all night, but they all quickly brushed him off.

As he too fell out onto the street, Giles felt a familiar creeping feeling of emptiness. The evening had been fun, but now what? A few hours sleep at most and then back to work? Giles thought of his empty house in Snaresbrook. A taxi out there would be £50 a least. He pictured himself fumbling for his keys, letting himself in and the cold and stale air of his place, the silence engulfing. He'd stumble onto the bed, probably still dressed, then wake up with the already creeping pain in his head matured into a full-blown hangover. Same hangover, different day.

Maybe it was the booze, but out here in among the tall City skyscrapers and the glass worked ornate buildings, he still felt totally alone. He'd feel just as alone at home. Worse even.

I know what you're thinking, Giles.

It had been a while since Giles had sex. And a lot longer since he'd curled up with a woman and just enjoyed the warmth as they'd both fallen asleep. Back at home were just dirty, cold sheets. It was no longer a home at all, just a place to sleep. He could barely stand the thought of it.

You know where to go, Giles.

He walked five minutes to Liverpool Street Station and hailed one of the few taxis still waiting for a late night fare.

"Mile End, the Station." The taxi driver didn't look back. He knew what that meant. And Giles knew he'd just added at least another £10 to his fare. Driver and passenger didn't speak for the journey.

Mile End. The class of girls there was far from the standard you get in Soho, but in the West End, the massage parlours were all run by pimps. Go through one of those little doors between smart coffee shops and gay bars around Windmill Street, up the stairs, and you didn't just get the girl, you got the hustle and the pressure.

You had to wait in some shabby room, listening to the girls, all screeching and crying in fake pleasure for the punter who'd got in before you. It was the pimps in charge in Soho and you better not put a foot wrong.

No, Mile End was better in that way. Things were a bit more fluid. A bit more *freelance.*

Entrepreneurial spirit, Giles. You got to hand it to them.

The cab pulled up about 100 metres after Mile End Tube Station. The meter said £17, though Giles handed over £30. He'd almost fallen asleep in the back, lulled by the movement of the cab as it swung round back roads to drive up the fare. He wished he'd told the taxi driver to take him home.

But you're here now, Giles. Get your money's worth.

It would still be another pile to get home afterwards. In for a penny.

At this time of night, the girls were confident enough to hang around the closed station. In the last few hours when Mile End was open, London Underground staff and the British Transport Police would wander around the foyer ostentatiously, driving the waiting girls onto the other side of the street, or to outside Turkish bars where the owners saw their presence as an extra service for the guys drinking inside. Sometimes for themselves, too.

Giles walked back towards the station, just about able to make brief eye contact with two girls under the street lamps, but keeping his head down – just going home, his gait said – then past three other less appealing, more *worn*, girls who were also waiting around.

Girls. That was stretching it, Giles thought as he made his first swipe past the station. He waited at the roadside, as if waiting for an opportunity to cross. The three he'd avoided were out, that was for sure. Haggard. Their hair already crumpled from too many tricks that night. The other two, well they were potentials. One - blonde she was, probably fake anyway - was dolled up nice enough and max about 30. Okay, maybe 35. There were crows' feet around her eyes, but she held his gaze strongly enough. She had a tight pink top pulled over large, obviously fake breasts.

No harm in that, Giles. A bit of body work. Obviously knows her way around this particular area.

The other had thin lips and tired eyes. She had no real breasts to speak of, but to be honest, there was no meat on her anywhere. She was pale and gaunt, not just thin. Giles hadn't seen her arms, but imagined what he might find there. Anyway, she'd turned away when Giles had looked towards her, wanting to avoid his connection.

Giles spun around, trying to give the impression he'd decided not to cross the road after all. He walked toward the blonde with the pink top. But she was already looking towards a Mercedes that had pulled up alongside, and dropped its passenger window. She strode over to it and started chatting to the driver inside.

Looks like a bit of charity work for the junkie Giles.

He turned again and moved towards the gaunt girl, coming up to stand next to her. Her brown hair was limp and greasy and fell down the back of her denim jacket. Her hands were spindly, and she messed with them uncomfortably; each of her nails had been bitten down to the bare skin. She stared down at the ground.

"Do you have somewhere to go?" he asked her in a flat voice.

"I don't take people home." She continued staring and was shivering as she spoke.

"Then where?"

"The park. I know a way in. It's private enough."

Still not looking up, she moved away from Giles and started towards the crossing where he had stood before. He followed her, a meter behind. Then they crossed the road and walked into the shadows cast by the head-height hedges surrounding Mile End Park.

"Fifty pounds," she said. "Straight up sex, nothing... nothing *more*."

"I've got £35."

"Forty."

Done, Giles, you filthy fucker.

He kept walking with her, indicating his consent. At the corner of the park, where a street light had gone out, there was a gap in the fence and the hedge that had obviously once been filled by a tree that was no longer there. As soon as they were on the other side, she waited, still staring at the ground. He pulled out two twenty-pound notes.

She'll be out of here and straight onto her dealer for another hit. No questions asked. Just give me the money, then hand me a needle and a teaspoon.

Ten minutes later Giles had left the park, barely able to hold in his need to throw up.

He'd used the girl, plain and simple. No, it was worse. He'd pushed her further than she had wanted to go.

"Nothing *more*," she had said.

He'd ignored it. He'd tried to imagine she was Lisa. In their shared bed. Warmth surrounding them.

The woman had lain there limply. Giles had asked her to hug him. She'd put her arms around him, but Giles had told her to pull him tight. She did, but without conviction.

He just wanted to recreate what he'd had. To feel something like when he made love to Lisa.

And when he'd felt nothing, he'd pushed the young woman's arms above her head.

It only took her to say 'no, don't' once for Giles to be reminded of how Lisa would pretend to resist.

He'd finished, and within seconds reality had sprung back. He realised he was lying above a woman he didn't know. On dank, damp grass, surrounded by used condoms and empty beer cans. And he had ignored this vulnerable young woman's request for him to stop.

"No, don't," she had said. It wasn't to titillate him like Lisa would. It was to refuse him.

The dead, lifeless feeling in the pit of Giles' stomach had come immediately. Before, he had felt a few minutes' rush of paying a woman for sex. Only now, afterwards, the depression felt far deeper. Far more painful. Far lonelier.

Idiot. You fucking shit.

He hadn't been able to see her face in the dark. Only the outline of her stick thin body and her twiggy arms.

What was he doing there, in some fucking park in the dark, in the shitty east end of London? What the hell was *she* doing here? What was she, 22, 23, and already a junky selling herself to sleaze bags like him?

She should have known better than to trust a prick like him.

Stupid, stupid fucking whore. Stupid, stupid fucking prick.

"Sorry," he had said. "So, sorry," as if he could take it all back. Erase.

His standing had allowed a shaft of light to emerge through the bushes and onto her face. Her eyes were puffed up - the most astoundingly marine-green - glossy with tears.

Giles had reached into his pocket and pulled out every note he had there. Twenty pounds, maybe £30. He held them out to her, and she had turned her head away from him.

"Take it."

She had reached up and snatched the notes quickly.

"It's just... I'm sorry."

Giles turned and walked away, keeping his head low and in the shadows. As he ducked through the hole in the fence, he looked momentarily back in the girl's direction. He could see the soles of her bare feet as she knelt low and away from him. She was reaching into the scrub, trying to find her shoes in the deep dark bushes.

He hesitated for a moment. And then he left, more angry with himself than he had ever been.

You need to be punished Giles. Someone needs to be punished.

33

Benny felt an unwelcome light seeping behind his eyelids, the morning switch-on of the chamber lights rousing him. Just a few minutes more.

Benny half-drifted off again, feeling an almost-unconscious hope he'd felt every morning that this nightmare would be over. But he felt the hardness of the step beneath his face, the painful creases in his body as it folded itself in and out of the steps he was lying on. The disappointment pulled him fully back into consciousness.

Benny watched the orange glow behind his eyelids again, then reached across and gently touched Megan's side. He could feel the gentle rise and fall of her body, and he felt secure that she was still there.

He saw the dark descending over the orange glow and almost mistook it for sleep returning. But the shadow was moving around.

He opened his eyes just in time to see a huge footprint descending from above him before it connected with his face, crushing his nose and sending blood spurting across his cheeks. The sharp pain sprung him into alertness and through eyes blurry from pain and the wetness of his blood he saw Giles raising his boot for another strike.

"Cable ties," shouted Giles. "Fucking cable ties. Is that the best you can do?"

Help him out, Giles. Release Benny from this spiral.

Benny leapt into a seated position and threw his face, along with what could only be a broken nose, between his knees. His face was protected, but he felt the heavy boot crash down onto the back of his head. It was the exact spot where he'd hit the wall two days before, and the excruciating pain again sent ripples of agony around his skull that were so fierce that his ears rang. He watched as blood from his nose spattered into the step ahead of him.

"Giles, no. We can work this out," screamed Megan.

"Shut up. You're next, after I've released him."

"Released him? What do you mean?"

"Megan, go. Quickly, go," Benny said.

In one movement, Benny stood on his still painful leg and pushed Megan further up the steps. He swung round towards Giles, who was just a step or two below him. He was holding one of Benny's steel toe capped work boots in both hands. It was covered in the builder's blood.

The fingers on Giles' left hand were blistered and red, a stripe of red ran down the man's hands and into his wrist.

Giles had used his lighter to burn through the plastic cable ties Benny had taken from his work, and that he'd used to secure Giles' hands together during the night. The crazy bastard had burned his own hands to release the plastic ties, then burned through the shoe laces tied around his ankles too.

A lighter. A fucking lighter. First thing to be taken off a prisoner when they come in.

Benny looked again. There were cigarette burns on the

back of the man's hands. Classic self harm. Classic voices. Classic build up to a psychotic episode.

Giles - or whatever Giles had become - had been planning this all night. Preparing himself, punishing himself, using the cigarette pain to prepare himself for what was to come.

The light. And the advantage of surprise.

"I have to release you, Benny. You and Megan. It's for your own good. Release you from this place."

Giles lashed out again with the boot, catching the bigger man squarely in his chest.

Benny stumbled back, his injured right foot hitting the step above, twisting again and sending a forceful ripple of pain up through his ankle, then his knee. It buckled with the force.

He could hear Megan screeching just above him as he saw Giles' shadow retreating down some steps. Benny took a moment to assess the damage Giles had inflicted.

His head felt like it was going to explode. The pulsating pain of the back of his head and the sharp stabbing pain where his nose was broken felt like they were pressing in on his brain, squeezing it like a vice.

The tie on his right ankle had come away, and it felt as if it had been smashed with a lump hammer. And now his knee felt cracked. He heard it grind as he attempted to swing it from side to side. His eyes were streaming with blood and tears. And he had no boots on.

"Giles, please," said Benny, but his voice came out like a gurgle. He spat blood that had dribbled down into his mouth from the front and down the back of his throat.

No choice now. Benny knew it had to come down to him and Giles, and if he didn't put Giles seriously out of action then what: another boot in the face during the night? Megan left totally alone with this man?

He still felt sympathy for Giles. The man in grief for his wife. The man depressed by his job. The man who suffered from voices telling him to do despicable things.

But now the rules had changed. His attempt to tie Giles up for his own safety had failed. There was no choice now but to take the guy down.

Benny didn't kid himself; he was already at a serious disadvantage. He gripped the bannister and pulled himself upright. He stepped with his damaged right foot onto the level below towards Giles, but the pain was excruciating in his ankle and his knee.

There was no power in his leg at all, and certainly not enough to lever him down the stairs. Instead, he hovered his right in the air and hopped down with the left. First one step, then another, then another, then one more before he had to take a rest.

His eyes clearing now, he could see Giles five steps below him, still holding the boot in his hands. Benny quickly covered three more steps, hopping on his left. But with every step, Giles backed down one more. He was playing with him, wearing him down.

Benny covered his chest as Giles moved back towards him, expecting another blow from the boot. But he felt a sharp punch in the stomach. He stumbled backwards, his painful right foot hitting the ground to prevent him from tumbling down the stairs. The same move that had twisted his foot two days ago.

Another shock of pain rose from the foot and enveloped his whole body. Benny grabbed the rail tighter and hopped down one more step towards Giles.

He was ready for another punch this time. He ducked to

the left just in time to prevent Giles landing a direct hit. Instead, the fist brushed his shoulder, which held firm.

Benny looked up, and for the first time saw clearly enough to register Giles' features. His face was twisted between anger and determination, shock and fear.

The man wasn't sure himself what he was doing.

And he was crying.

"I have to release you, Benny. Don't you understand? I'm a useless pile of shit. The best I can do is to release you from this hell."

Benny hesitated, then shook his head. No, there could be no reasoning with this man. He used the half-beat of Giles' confusion to land a hard left punch into his face. As Giles bent over with the pain, gasping for the breath that had just been taken out of him, Benny punched again. This time a cuff around his head.

He watched his opponent rock to the side. His head hit the wall and he stumbled backwards, only just managing to steel himself against the metal bannister.

Benny hopped again and this time, slamming his now painful right foot down into the step for leverage, planted his fist into Giles' face. This time it was Giles' turn for his face to explode in a bloody mess. Benny had missed his nose, but split his lip badly and splashed his blood over his chin and cheeks.

But Giles was still quicker. Benny's dead weight, now heaving from exhaustion, moved down the steps further towards him. Benny had the advantage of height, but Giles had already come in with an almighty tackle, headfirst into his stomach. Benny was winded, but didn't go down.

Ending up on his knees, Giles raised Benny's boot again, and brought it down in an audible crack onto Benny's left foot. They both watched as Benny's toes bent against the sharp edge of the step. Now both of his feet were out of action.

He was going to lose this.

Now Benny didn't need to rest, he needed to get away. Lumbering, he stumbled back up the steps on his heels, step after step, never taking his eye off Giles, who was straightening up again, wiping blood from his face. With two feet out of action and Giles still having the boot, what hope did he have?

Scrambling backwards, the heel of Benny's twisted right foot slipped on the edge of a step and failed to connect with the one below. It sent him reeling backwards, too quickly for Benny to reach out and grab the rail. He felt his spine hit the edge of another step and heard a terrible cracking as one of his vertebrae exploded.

Benny didn't have time to feel the pain. A moment later, the back of his head hit a step. A direct hit where he'd already smashed it two days ago, and Giles had redone the damage two minutes ago. This time his skull gave way, his neck was forced forwards and his chin hit his chest in an impossible position.

Rachel was lying in bed next to him, breathing in and out gently, staring at the ceiling with a smile on her face. The tourniquet was loose but still around her arm. It was the last thought Benny had.

34

_____

Even as Megan ran up the stairs, she knew how futile it would be. She had an endless spiral to run up, but she had nowhere to go. Eventually she was going to tire. She already felt as weak as she'd ever been. And when she did stop, he'd be upon her. He'd be much faster than she, and he still had shoes on.

She climbed steps until she could climb no more. There was silence from below. Then the smell of cigarette smoke. Giles now had one more left, if she'd counted correctly.

The man was in no rush. He knew exactly what she did. They had all the time in the world. The cigarettes calmed him, she thought. After the battle with Benny below, he was taking a moment to regroup.

Rethink, perhaps?

If so, only for a time. Then the voices would be back.

Megan needed to pee. She needed to drink too. It reminded her of the lipstick cap she'd peed into a few hundred steps from here.

And then she thought of something else. Something her Dad had given her. The thing she had decided she would not pee in. It was still there, tucked into her bra where no one else had seen it.

It was the one thing she hadn't turned out onto the step all those days ago.

She shook her head.

I take decisions and act on them.

She hadn't used those words in her interview. Back then it was meaningless drivel, to get the job done. Like Dad said.

Now they felt totally and completely necessary.

———

As she stepped down towards where the smoke was wafting up, Megan had one hope and one hope only.

That Giles wasn't looking in her direction.

Her feet, in torn tights, padded silently back the twenty steps to where they had all made their home. The detritus of their lives. The broken light socket. The bloodied tie. Her shoes and Benny's boots, one now also covered in blood.

She peeked her head around the curve and was pleased to see Giles was facing down the steps towards Benny. Her friend's twisted body lay like a barrier across the spiral staircase, as if it were a dam preventing anything else from tumbling down.

She got as close to Giles' back as she could, knowing that eventually he would hear her. Whether his face was kind or angry, it could no longer matter.

There was only one way out of this.

I use my initiative, act quickly when the circumstances require it.

She heard Giles breathe heavily. He flicked the cigarette butt down the stairs, past where Benny lay.

"It wasn't my fault," he said. "He slipped. I didn't kill him on purpose. He needed to be released from the staircase."

For a moment, she wondered whether he was talking to himself. Mumbling like he had been for the last two days.

But he turned.

He looked up at her from where he sat.

"The voices? Can you understand that? I didn't mean for this to happen."

Megan's heartbeat slowed. He truly meant what he said.

"I've lost everything," Giles said. "And now, this. I deserve everything I get."

Megan reconsidered. The man was so vulnerable. It wasn't his fault. Benny's death. The spiral. His mental illness. Even Lisa leaving him.

All of our lives are shaped for us, by our genes, by our brains, by our innate faults, by our upbringing, everything we encounter along the way. Where was fault when there were so many factors at play?

Was Megan really responsible for Rachel getting hurt? For her leaving the college? Was Megan responsible for her own father's neglect? Her mother, for leaving him, maybe creating the man he had become?

"Giles, it's going to be okay," she said finally. "Whatever happens, it's going to be okay."

He shook his head.

She sat six steps above him, her resolve run out as the man began to weep below her.

She watched as it transformed into heaving tears. And then something else.

What was it? A slight ticcing in his neck.

"Shut up," he said.

"Giles," said Megan, her heart beating quicker again.

"Fuck off. Leave it, lads, fucking leave it."

"Giles," Megan shouted. "Come back to me."

"It's okay," he said. "It's okay. No, fuck off. Fuck off."

"Oh Giles," Megan cried. "Oh poor, poor Giles."

"Fuck off."

The man was crying, fiercely fighting the voices in his head. Drowning.

"Oh Giles, oh Giles, I'm so sorry."

"Sorry," he said, his neck fully ticcing now. "Sorry, sorry. Fuck off, lads. Sorry, sorry."

His face ticced as he appeared to try to shake off the storm.

Megan stood, knowing there could be no other choice.

"I'm sorry I have to do this, Giles," she said. She pulled out the small liquid chilli spray her Dad had made for her and insisted she carried at all times. Highly illegal, but highly effective, he'd say.

She walked down two steps, held out the spray, and pumped it four times directly into Giles' face.

The man screamed in agony, turning to face away, bringing his arms over his face, scratching at his eyes to take away the sting. He stood slightly, grasping the bannister, trying to shake away the pain.

Megan kicked Giles firmly in the back. His feet slipped, and he lost his balance, falling forward, tumbling over. His face his the stone steps below.

"Oh God," Megan screeched. "I'm sorry Giles, I'm so sorry."

The man writhed upside down on the staircase, trying to reach for his eyes again. His arms were trapped by his own body.

Giles cried out, screeching with the pain of his now broken cheekbone and the seething agony in his eyes.

Dad had taught her rubbing your eyes only made it

worse. You needed to wash chilli out with water or prefer-ably milk, yogurt even.

"Ah, my eyes, you didn't have to. Let me release you, Megan. I need to help you out of this place."

She'd got the advantage she needed. Megan just needed to know how injured Giles had been in the fall.

He screeched as he yanked an arm from under his body and tried to lift it onto a step, attempting to swivel his body upright.

As he turned, Megan saw his face streaming. She saw cheeks burning with the chilli, but with anger too.

"I'm going to kill you, Megan," said Giles. So quietly, and gently, he might have been talking to children. "There's nothing left for either of us down here. I have to release you, and then I'm going to kill myself."

He attempted to pull himself up by the banister, but his foot slipped and Giles let out a little cry.

It emboldened Megan.

"I'd prefer it the other way up," said Megan. For a moment she imagined it was one of those films, like The Running Man, or Highlander or The Hunger Games.

Last one to survive discovers it's all a trick. God, she hoped this was some kind of sick game show.

She steeled herself for the last battle. What did she have: Benny's boots, a little more chilli spray, the advantage of being above him?

There was no way Giles was going to let her tie him up again. The man had burned his own skin to get free.

She quickly dismissed the horrific idea of bashing Giles' head in with the boots. She didn't have the stomach for it, and her sympathy for the man remained. Even now he shouldn't have to die that way.

What did Giles have: a lighter, a last cigarette, a pathological ability to destroy, and the support of the voices in his head cheering him on.

She knew she had the disadvantage, physically and mentally.

She backed up the stairs, watching Giles carefully as he struggled onto his feet. He was obviously slowed by an injury, but how bad it wasn't clear.

For the moment, he continued to be calm. Considered even. He became the Giles she'd known on the first day.

"Megan," he said, "that chilli hurts like hell. If you have to use it again, I understand. I need you to know that. None of this is your fault. It's mine. You should do what you have to do."

She hesitated.

"I understand," she said.

He held up a last cigarette.

"Last one," he said, flicking the lighter. "You want a few drags?"

"No, thanks. Take it slowly, Giles. Enjoy it. Give me some distance, please?"

He smiled. "Here," he called.

He threw the lighter up to her. It rested on a step just above. A little more advantage to her.

"I'm going to go now, Giles," she said. "Take as long as you can with that fag."

He waved it at her.

"See you around," he smiled.

Megan walked backwards up the staircase.

Megan tried to think tactically. She had calmed Giles, and he'd given her some advantage and attempted to disarm himself.

As she climbed a few steps, she looked around her. He would expect her to climb far above. Keep going, getting as far away as she could.

She stopped just two twists around the spiral, about twelve steps. This was where it had all began. The light fitting was still hanging loose from the concrete five further steps up. The footprints, dirt, litter they'd all left. Her empty lipstick. Benny's boots. A pen and a pencil.

They'd slept here. Talked here. Disagreed here. Comforted. Even joked.

She lay a boot down on a step. Backed up another two and lay another boot down. She backed up another few steps and lay the bottle down. It contained just a few finger nail's worth of Dad's chilli spray.

She backed up again and looked around at the light fitting. If she could reach up, there would be just enough room in the hole for her to squeeze her fingers through. She could use it as a swinging position, giving her more sturdiness to kick out with her legs.

Silently, she moved back down the steps to Benny's first boot. She picked it up, pressed on the toe cap to feel the solidity of the steel beneath. She pushed her hand into the boot, as if it were a boxing glove. She picked up a pen in her left hand and mimicked stabbing motions.

She took a deep breath, and could still smell the cigarette rising from beneath. Not yet, she thought.

But soon.

35

The smell of smoke petered out. Megan waited, listening for any movement from below. It was ten minutes before she thought she heard slow but loud footsteps coming up the stairs.

It was almost as if Giles was warning her, still fighting the voices even now. Doing what he could with his body to fight his confused mind.

"Fuck off, fuck off." She heard Giles ticcing down below. "She's okay. Fuck off, lads. She's my friend."

A little cry from Giles, as he lifted himself up on one leg, obviously using the banister to climb slowly. Resisting, she imagined, at every step.

Two more steps, she decided. Two more steps and she would have to go on the attack.

"Fuck off."

Step.

"No, I'm going back. Fuck off.

Step.

Was that a step down or up?

"Shit," said Megan.

She stood, her heart beating, visions of her Dad scolding her, throwing plates across the room, accusing her of being lazy, or selfish, or dressing like a whore.

She stiffened her arms, ready to start the assault.

When Giles eventually came around the spiral below her, it was as if he was keeping his head low. Limping up on one foot. He didn't want to see her first. After everything, he was still doing his best to give Megan her best first shot.

This, Dad, is for a girl who will never make anything of herself.

She launched down the stairs, and punched Giles in the back of the head with the steel toe capped boot. At the same time, she pushed the pen into the back of his neck.

Giles' head took the boot blow, and bounced lightly off the tiled wall. The pen scratched his neck, but didn't penetrate. Giles bent over with the pain, and Megan kicked out frantically, sending Giles falling backwards down the steps again.

She screeched herself, unable to believe what she'd just done. She threw the boot down after him, hoping to connect with his head. It bounced on concrete and fell down a few steps more.

She heard an almighty cry out from below.

"Bitch."

She knew Giles was no longer in control. She backed up the steps and took the other boot onto her right hand.

"Don't you come near me," Megan hollered, though that was exactly what she wanted him to do. If he could.

She heard a growl, then laboured single hops up the steps, slightly quicker than they had been before. This time, Giles was face up and she could see blood running from his left ear, where the boot had connected.

She looked into his eyes. There was barely anything of Giles left. Just his demons.

She stepped down again, swing the boot. This time Giles could see it coming and put up an arm to prevent the blow. His forearm took the power of the toecap, hurting him but not breaking anything. Giles stayed in place, still grasping the bannister.

He came up one more step. Megan tried to swing again, but she was losing power in her arms and any chance of getting him off guard. Catching a final limp throw of her right hand, Giles grabbed the boot and snatched it from her hand.

He was going to use that boot to batter her to death.

Giles shook his head fiercely. He turned and threw the boot as far down the staircase as he could.

"Go," he said.

Megan retreated more steps up and took up the chilli spray.

"Fuck off."

"That's it Giles, you tell them."

"Fucking bitch. Fucking Asswipe."

She watched him shake his head again and then lurch upwards. Megan leant down and sprayed a mist of chilli liquid all around. She couldn't get close enough to Giles' face this time, but she attempted to create a barrier at least.

She watched as the pink droplets fell in the air, some falling onto Giles' clothing, but most onto the steps. He'd closed his eyes to protect them, and she came down a step and kicked out, catching him in the shoulder holding the banister.

Giles fell backwards, but caught the bannister again with his other hand. He moved one step up again, this time with more determination.

She turned and ran another three or four steps up, turned and looked up, wildly trying to find the light fitting.

She reached up onto her tiptoes and had to stretch forward to put her fingers into the concrete hole. It could only be one movement, a swing forward because she wasn't tall enough to reach the roof on flat feet.

Still watching Giles as he recovered from her last blow, she fumbled for a good grip.

Her hand brushed the screwdriver Benny had left up there, jammed into the bulb connection. She briefly thought about what Benny had said about the danger of electrocution.

She dug her fingers into the hole where the bulb had been and braced herself to swing.

When it came, it was with a cry of anger and frustration from Giles. He leapt out from the bannister, as if to grab her waist and pull her down.

She launched into the air, connecting both feet with the man's head. But it was only a brush, and her bare feet failed to connect as solidly as she'd hoped.

Megan clung onto the hole in the concrete and frantically kicked out. Her feet connected a few times, before she felt them suddenly jerk from under her. Her fingers slipped from the roof, and she fell painfully onto an arm, which caught the edge of a step.

On her way down, she'd caught the wires of the light, dislodged the connection and plunged them both into total darkness.

She tried to kick out again, but now Giles had grabbed both of her ankles. She felt his fingers tighten before he dragged her down. She felt the incredible pain as her spine and head bumped down the steps. Her skirt rode up her legs against the steps, and she felt her blouse tear, then the skin of her back graze deeply against the concrete.

No, not here. Not like this.

She tried to wiggle her legs, but they barely moved as Giles moved up her body. She crossed her legs tightly, preventing her biggest fear now that Giles had the advantage.

"It's no use now," Giles whispered. But was that a tremble behind his voice? "I'm here now, I have to end it for both of us."

For a moment, she felt relieved. At least he would not rape her. She knew Giles was fighting that inside. She thanked God he was winning.

She felt Giles' hands as they found her neck; his tears falling onto her face.

"I'm sorry, Megan," Giles was crying loudly, as he mumbled the words.

"It's no use resisting. It's what I have to do. I need to release you. I'm sorry, Lisa... Megan. This is what they've done to me."

But Giles was heaving with sobs, and Megan noticed a relaxation in his body, a slight releasing of the grip around her neck.

Her fear abated for a few seconds, enough for her to understand what she needed to do.

"No, Giles," she said in as calm a voice as she could muster. "You don't have to do this." She felt more sobbing and more pressure released on her neck.

"Stop, Giles. Stop and let me hold you. I'm here for you."

"Oh, Lisa."

Megan felt her neck come free. It sickened her to do it, but she relaxed her arms from pushing against his shoulders.

"That's right. Let me hold you," she said. "They did this to you, Giles. You are better than them."

She tried to prevent herself from retching as she wrapped her arms around his shoulders. Pulled his body onto her chest, his head next to hers. The pressure on her neck released completely now as his body shook uncontrollably.

"Oh Lisa," Giles whispered between sobs. "Oh Lisa, I'm so sorry."

Megan patted him, whispered back even though bile was rising in her throat. "It's okay now, Giles, I'm here."

"They fucking destroyed me," Giles cried. "They destroyed me, and Lisa left. And now there's nothing."

"There's life, Giles. It's going to be okay."

"There is nothing, I'm nothing," Giles' tears had stopped. "We're down here in this fucking hole and nothing matters. I have to release you."

Megan felt pressure on her neck again, pushing her again towards the stone. "Nothing matters now. Nothing mattered before. Everything's gone."

This time the pressure on her neck became strong enough that Megan started to choke. She tried to call out, but the sound got caught in her throat. For a moment, she couldn't breathe.

And if she couldn't breathe, she couldn't talk Giles down. She couldn't pretend to be Lisa.

Megan's fear was now replaced by her feeling that she needed to draw in air. The pain of Gile's hands around her neck had dissipated. Now her lungs burned and her head began to fug over.

She knew suddenly it would have to go this way.

It was time to do it, or give up.

Megan lifted her arms as high as they would go behind Giles' back, as if reaching out for the end to come. As she felt her eyes rising up into her forehead, she had just one thought.

Dad.

She held both her hands as tightly as she could around the handle of the screwdriver in her hands. So tightly every muscle in her arms hurt, and it took every ounce of remaining power in her body to pull the tool towards her.

Up into Giles' back.

She let out a final urgent scream; one of terror, determination, and hope as the blade connected. The sensation in her hands was sickening as she felt the screwdriver break through the skin. She could hear the cracking as the screwdriver blade scraped against one of Gile's ribs. She almost retched as the bone splintered and the blade broke through and plunged into the mush behind. Organs, skin, blood.

Giles let out a huge shriek, followed immediately by a gurgled cry which could only have been blood rising in his throat. He immediately released the pressure on Megan's neck, and she gulped heavily for air.

Giles let out a deep cough and Megan felt a sticky and warm liquid spatter her face and get into her mouth. She breathed in again, and the oxygen brought her back to full awareness.

She wrenched her arms away from his back, leaving the screwdriver where it had found a home. Giles was moaning through bubbling, urgent breaths. She could feel blood soaking the sides of his shirt and sticking her blouse to her own skin.

Her hands felt slick and tacky. At once, she pulled her

elbows up, connected her palms to each of his shoulders, and pushed as hard as she could while twisting her body from beneath him. Her spine was in agony again and she scraped herself back up one step, then another, eventually getting high enough to pull her legs out from underneath him.

With both her bare feet, she kicked out desperately in the dark. For a beat she listened and heard only a very low gurgle from Giles. She stood, listened for the gurgle again, and grabbing the rail, kicked hard in its direction.

It connected with Giles somewhere, and she heard him tumble backwards down the steps. He cried out as each step damaged a different part of his body. Finally, she heard him come to rest.

In the pitch dark, she listened, catching her breath and weeping. She felt for the step in front of her, got her balance, and then ran upwards. Three steps, five, ten, fifteen. She didn't care that her toes stubbed and scraped painfully with every footfall. She didn't notice that she was crying hysterically, screaming with every step.

Megan kept running, though her thighs burned and the adrenaline in her blood stream leaked away, leaving only pain. It seemed to come from every part of her body: her feet, her legs, her lungs from screaming and desperate breathing, her back from where she knew her skin must be hanging in strips, her neck which felt burned and bruised. She had to keep going, pushing her body to the very limit.

The screwdriver had connected, that was for sure. The blood was proof of that. And the gurgling. But that meant nothing. It could have just been a superficial wound, lots of blood, but not much impact. Or maybe he was down there now, already lifeless.

Dead, thanks to her.

In the darkness, Megan became aware that she had stopped running. She realised she'd been walking upwards for the last few moments. Now she stopped completely.

Had she killed him? God, she hadn't *tried* to kill him. She didn't have a choice. It was all so fast, almost instinctive. She tried to calm her breathing and when that didn't work, she held her breath, feeling her heart pulsating wildly in her chest. But there was no sound from below. She let out a breath, breathed in, and held it again. Still no movement, no breath, no gurgling.

She'd killed him. The realisation took the wind out of her; she blew out air desperately and pointlessly looked around in panic in the dark.

No, she wouldn't go into a panic attack now.

She refused.

She was going to beat it. No more bin.

She tried to concentrate on the pain in her body, pushing away the panic in her head. Ten minutes ago, Giles was fighting his own mental urges. Now she was fighting hers. She was a murderer. He was lying below in a pool of his own blood, seeping from the puncture she had torn into his back.

Megan leaned over and pulled her body close to her legs, hugging them to her chest. She pushed her face into her knees and cried with both relief and grief for what she had done.

36

When he came for her it was all at once. It wasn't a leg grasp like ten minutes before. Without a sound, Giles leapt and landed on Megan's curled up body.

That's it, Giles, creep up on her. Finish what you started.

Giles had tried to reach around his back to find where the screwdriver was still jammed in. But whichever hand he used, he couldn't grasp it. She's stabbed me. I'm going to die down here.

Yeah, she's stabbed you, that's true. Ha ha, can't win them all Giles. But you can still go out with a bang, mate.

No! Giles stopped reaching behind him. He slowly climbed the staircase, led by her sobs. I'll be dead in ten minutes, twenty at best. She'll be left down here in this fucking pit. Alone, starving, scared. I need to... help.

Give me a fucking break, Giles. Help! You're in no position to help, old boy. Yeah, you could even say you're 'screwed' with that tool in your back.

No.

Yeah, like you helped that whore last night. She took a bit of slapping around too, didn't she, Giles? A bit of push and shove, to get what you needed.

It's over for all of us.

It's not over, Giles. This is us. Work hard, play hard. This is what we do.

It's not what I do. It's not what I DO!

Giles fell upon Megan and held her tight in his arms. Before she could fight him off, he pulled her on top of him and locked his hand over her mouth. He held tight, then rocked them both on the step, feeling the screwdriver embedded in his lower back, but without any pain.

He cried as he drifted his other arm up towards her neck. She tried to pull his arm down, but she had no energy to even get a hold. He rocked and cried and pulled his arm tighter.

"I'm sorry Megan," he said between sobs. "I'm sorry Lisa."

Faintly he could hear her breath catching, trying to cry out but not having the energy to do it. Her neck was in the crook of his elbow now, and he took more leverage to pull his hand up towards his own shoulder, squeezing.

There was no longer room for breathing. He kept on squeezing until long after she'd stopped trying to resist. Until long after her grip had released and her arms had fallen away.

37

As carefully as possible, Giles rolled Megan off his body and lowered her down on to the steps. He felt around for her arms, trying to manoeuvre her into a sleeping position. A peaceful one. With hands now drying with his own blood. He stroked her hair.

From his pocket, he took out a small black canister. In the dark, he counted each one of the 12 pills. He pushed them into his mouth, used his own blood as lubrication to swallow them one by one.

Then he wrapped his arms around his knees and pulled them close. He could still feel the pressure of the tool in his back and the taste the pills and the blood in his mouth. He stared into the pure blackness beyond, listening for the voices in his head to return.

Nothing.

"Nothing to say now, lads?" he shouted into the darkness, spitting out phlegm. "All quiet suddenly? Too much for you?"

He listened for the voices.

Nothing.

He rocked on his step, in time with his shallow soft breathing, trying to comfort himself.

He wanted to feel as he had when Lisa would hold him in bed. Back when they first got together. And for a moment he could feel her warmth. His eyes felt heavy, and he could no longer tell whether he'd closed them or not. He rocked slower and felt the welcome weight of a blackness.

A blackness that was even deeper than the surrounding darkness.

38

"**Y**ou okay, mate?"

Giles looked up from where he was sitting. In front of him was a middle-aged man with a bald head. Giles stared at him.

"Mate, you okay?"

Giles looked around him. The lights were on and there was a buzz of movement in the air. Deep below him, further down the steps, he heard a whoosh and a braking noise, the muffled sound of an announcer. He looked up from where he was sitting and the man had an impatient but puzzled look on his face.

"Yeah," he said to the man. "I'm fine. Just, I, I don't know, it's fine." Giles grabbed the bannister and pulled himself to standing. He concentrated on the sensations in his back, but there was nothing. In one hand there was a near-empty bottle of Lucozade.

"Okay, as long as you're sure," the bald-headed guy carried on up the stairs.

The lights. Giles looked up and saw the neat row of lit bulbs going down into the distance and around the spiral.

He put one foot down onto the step below him and the ease with which he did it surprised him. There was no aching in his legs, and the dead feeling of hunger in his stomach had gone. He swallowed and felt dry, but not the coarse, dryness of absolute desperate thirst. There was a dull ache in his head and a low nausea in his stomach.

Giles took more steps down, turning around the corner below, and saw a brighter rectangle of light open up before him. And through the rectangle, there were no more steps. The corridor stretched out flat into the distance. As he took his last step off the staircase and placed his foot onto the flat ground, he felt euphoria mixed with the dizzying unsteadiness of stepping off a rocking boat onto dry land.

He'd forgotten to take his meds yet again. Last night, with another night out. And then again this morning. He felt in his pocket. He always kept a spare blister for just this scenario.

Giles looked around and steadied himself against the wall. He saw a Tube train filled with strange faces. Around the corner, more commuters were climbing aboard the train. As they did, Giles walked, mesmerised, along the platform. He looked up at the blinking sign, indicating the train was headed for Morden. As the doors beeped, he noticed a young girl in a smart blouse and A-line skirt dip onto the train just as they were closing.

He headed to the other end of the platform, where a blue Way Out sign pointed off to the right. There, a greying older man in a faded blazer reached the bottom of the staircase, followed by a man in grubby jeans who looked up at the next train indicator board. The carriage screeched as it exited the station. A large tourist, with a huge sized suitcase emerged from the staircase, took out a hankie, and wiped his head. He heaved out a sigh, then headed for the platform too.

At the turn, Giles hesitated for a moment as he saw stairs leading up. But then he watched others going up and down the half-dozen steps, then carry on forward on the flat. He took the steps and allowed himself to be carried along with the crowd as it turned through corridors, eventually reaching the bottom of a long escalator. He hesitated again, then stepped onto the moving steps. He stood on the right, instead of his usual habit of following the keener commuters walking up on the left.

At the top, he saw the exit of ticket barriers and instinctively reached into his pocket to find his pass. He heard an inspector call for tickets and passes. It was there with his wallet, as he would normally have expected it to be.

He swiped and walked past a small shop and cash machines, then up another short flight of steps into the daylight. It wasn't a sunny day. It was grey and there was a wetness in the air, as if rain had just come or was about to start.

Giles took an enormous gulp, relishing the feeling of taking new air down into his lungs. There was no pain in his breath, no gurgling in his throat. The air tasted gritty and grey.

It tasted like London.

Giles sucked in more and more. Cars and busses and taxies queued at traffic lights, while other vehicles crept by in the other direction, cyclists swung among the vehicles and over crossings.

Dozens, perhaps hundreds, of people were walking this way and that, chatting or talking or striding ahead purposefully. Some were eating sandwiches from Sainsburys and Pret a Manger, a late breakfast grabbed on the way to work or a meeting. Over the road, two police officers were offering directions to a small group of Japanese tourists.

Giles looked down and saw a pile of free Metro newspapers. A man in blue was handing them out to anyone who would take one. It was the late edition. On the cover a passport-sized photograph caught his eye. He lifted a paper off the pile and leant against a wall to read.

The picture was of a young girl, plain but beautiful. It was only a minor story, a couple of column inches.

Suicide: police appeal

The City of London was brought to a standstill this morning, as emergency services dealt with a person on the line on the London Underground between Bank and St Paul's Stations.

A young woman named by police as Rachel Colly, 25, is thought to have stepped onto the tracks in the early hours of this morning. Police say her death is not being treated as suspicious. Her family have been informed.

In a statement issued this morning, The Metropolitan Police have said they would like to trace Ms Colly's movements in the 24 hours before the incident. They have appealed for anyone who may have seen or interacted with her during the previous day or night to come forward.

The Northern Line and Central Line experienced severe delays this morning, and Underground staff say parts of the track may be closed until the end of the day.

Giles stared into the marine-green eyes of the girl in the picture, nausea rising in his stomach. He breathed in the

London air again and looked around him. Hundreds of people and dozens of cars. Everyone going about their normal lives. He could be one of them. He could walk away. Not even blink. Keep taking the meds.

He looked over again at the Japanese tourists, who were giving their thanks to the police officers.

Giles gripped his newspaper tightly as he waited for the lights to change.

Dear Valued Reader,

Thank you for reading this book.

I hope you have been entertained, perhaps challenged and that you would like to read more of my writing.

You can find out more about my books at www.gideon-burrows.com

It would make a real difference to me if you were able to please leave a **review** on your **social media**, share your **recommendation** with your friends, and please write an honest review on your **favourite book buying and review site**.

I have a free book for you, if you sign up to my monthly newsletter. Simply go to Free Future Shop at my website.

Gideon Burrows
www.gideon-burrows.com

FUTURE SHOP

From the award winning author of *Portico* and *The Illustrator's Daughter* comes another fast paced, chilling and challenging novel, that puts you center stage and asks: what if it happened to you?

London.

A massive explosion. A man left in a deep coma.

He can't see. He can't feel. He can't speak. He can't move.

But he can hear.

And amongst the noise of police investigations, press speculation, political disagreements and hospital squabbles, he discovers what happened.

And who was really to blame for the attack.

What he knows might bring justice. But at who's expense?

Please buy direct from the author

at www.gideon-burrows.com

ACKNOWLEDGMENTS

This book was only possible thanks to my valued Alpha and Beta readers who continue to support my work. And thanks to the wider independent writing community, of which I'm delighted to be a part.

Thanks also to Andy MacDonald and Kay Barrett for eagle eye proofreading. If you find any latent errors, please do email me at gideon@ngomedia.org.uk

ABOUT THE AUTHOR

Gideon Burrows is an award winning fiction and non-fiction writer.

He is author of the *Who's In Control?* series of novels, which aim to challenge the reader into considering what they would do in a terrifying or challenging situation. They include *The Spiral, The Illustrator's Daughter, Portico, and Future Shop.* He's currently working on the fifth book in the series.

Gideon was semi-finalist in the Kindle Book Awards for his social media thriller *Portico*, and winner of the Writing Magazine Self Published Book Award for his first non-fiction book, *Men Can Do it: Why Men Don't Do Childcare*.

He can be found at www.gideon-burrows.com, where you can join his mailing list and download the free book, *Martin & Me*, a difficult tale of a personal relationships, spying and the arms trade.

Age 13, Gideon thought he was going either going to be a writer or a ninja. His parents bought him a typewriter rather than a set of nunchucks, so that was that decided.

He trained as a journalist and spent 10 years writing for major UK newspapers and magazines.

Gideon is a qualified bicycle mechanic, a keen road cyclist and a fan of professional cycling. His fastest time for a 10 mile time trial is 25 minutes, dead on; and the climb of Sa Colobra in Majorca a not too bad 38 minutes, 28 seconds.

Not that he's counting.

Under a pen name, Gideon is writing a series of ninja themed action novels. His knowledge of the ancient ninja path may yet prevail...

Printed in Great Britain
by Amazon

10515314R10151